THE MAGIC KILLERS

Bronco Hammer

Sierra West Books

Invictus
Out of the night that covers me
Black as the pit from pole to pole,
I thank whatever gods may be
For my unconquerable soul.

In the fell clutch of circumstance,
I have not winced nor cried aloud.
Under the bludgeonings of chance
My head is bloody, but unbowed.

Beyond this place of wrath and tears
Looms but the Horror of the shade,
And yet the menace of the years
Finds, and shall find, me unafraid.

It matters not how strait the gate,
How charged with punishments the scroll,
I am the master of my fate
I am the captain of my soul.

WILLIAM ERNEST HENLEY (1849-1903)

CONTENTS

PROLOGUE

"Remain seated, if you dare, as we explore the darkest realms of the magical arts."

Nicolo DeCarlo looked sharp in his perfectly tailored tuxedo, patent leather oxford shoes, cape, and a dashing, yet mysterious, blood red fez. He is the hottest magician on the circuit and at the top of his game.

The crowd, taking a break from gambling in the casino, was raucously receptive to his show, especially when he flashed his satin cape and the two beautiful women appeared in dark red high-slit dresses with low-cut tops, as they seductively performed what might be described as a harem-girl routine, around the star of the show, Nicolo the Magnificent, Master of the Dark Arts. Or at least that what his headliner billing on a massive neon sign by the street declared. Becoming a hit celebrity as a magician, even at a regional level, is quite an accomplishment, especially for a retired cop.

Nicolo smiled and bowed, acknowledging the enthusiastic applause.

The drunken cheers and hoots from the audience bolstered the performers' enthusiasm. Nicolo waved his baton and the girls started tossing some ball-caps with cocktail coupons inside into the crowd... buy one - get one free, of course.

Raising his fist in the air, a puff of smoke covered the stage and when it cleared, the girls were gone and a man in a very realistic gorilla suit appeared on center stage, menacingly beating his chest and roaring.

The crowd gasped.

A woman screamed.

None of this is possible, how is he doing it?

Nicolo made a face like a school kid caught committing an addition error at the blackboard, then waved his baton again... another cloud of smoke appeared and the girls were back, but this time in cheerleader outfits.

The two gorgeous women led the loud and animated audience in a closing cheer as the curtain fell and at least a hundred balloons with the ubiquitous but coveted drink coupons attached dropped from the ceiling.

Nicolo smiled. This gig was so much better than writing traffic tickets in the heat, back in the old days on the police department. Beautiful girls, no drunk drivers vomiting in the back seat, and ice-cold air conditioning. A traffic officer's retirement dream.

But then one day it wasn't.

Something bad occurred... a missing friend, which happens. But this time there was a homicide involved.

The situation was serious enough that Nicolo, the Master of Dark Arts, made a call to his friend Becker, the master of busting heads.

CHAPTER 1 - BECKER

This is not my happy place.

I don't think it could be a happy place for anyone.

This is a bad place.

It is dark, dank, and miserable.

It is not the kind of place one would like to be murdered in, not that getting murdered anywhere is swell. But this isn't a murder... I hope... More likely, this is just one of those beat and release things.

Struggling seems pointless. There are three of them and one of me. Not great odds, not the worst odds, but... not ideal.

Yeah, I'm certain now. I don't want to be here.

Maybe it's that toxic bug spray odor lingering from the monthly exterminator visit. Or, perhaps it's the overall lack of modern ventilation as we know it. I suspect any flatulence released within this room since the place was built still remains intact, floating ethereally through the webs, dust, and mildew that provide all this medieval dungeon charm. Or, perhaps my lack of enthusiasm about this room might have something to do with these red paint stains. Some dumbass spilled red paint all over the floor.

That *is* paint, right?

Or maybe, just maybe, I'm not comfortable with these hostile pseudo-security men who are preparing to do me grievous bodily harm.

I'll admit, this sure looks like a good place for that kind of stuff, you know, violence, cruelty, and murder.

The room is dark, out of the way, and effuses all the charm of a clogged toilet in a Baltimore gas station bathroom. Every other square foot of this building is full of neon and noise, fun and games, booze and gluttony, sex and smoke... things that hold more appeal than this square concrete box with it's lone steel door, the rusty drain in the center of the floor, and the few odds and ends of junk laying about.

Is that a chain saw over there? Why would they have a... never mind. Forget I brought it up.

A voice from my left made an announcement. "Okay, asshole. We're going to have a talk."

I breathed in some stale storage room air while my eyes adjusted to what little light the red exit sign above the door and the dim florescent bulb hanging from the ceiling provided. Why would you bother putting an exit sign in a room with only one door? Probably some casino building code. Which makes me wonder, when did casinos start caring about building codes?

My 'hosts' are circling me now, moving slowly and sizing me up. That is never a good sign.

I noticed when we came in that the sign outside

the door in the hallway said storage. This might look like a storage room, but this was never a place for storage. Storage rooms have shelves. This room is bare bones. It is more likely used only as a place for talking... private talks. The type of talks that dish out a healthy serving of psychological abuse, with a side order of physical trauma included at no additional charge. I suspect that's what this is about.

We are in a casino... the happiest place on earth... isn't it? Maybe that's Orlando... for me, this is the *unhappiest* place on earth right now, or at least the unhappiest place in Broward County, Florida.

So why would a legitimate, but generally corrupt, fully licensed business need a 'storage' room without anything stored in it, you might ask. It's not complicated, really. In the casino business, an employee, customer, or vendor occasionally needs a serious talking to, especially those who display poor judgement or lack money management skills. The hoods call it a 'tune up.' On other occasions, they 'have a chat' with special fools, insiders and associates who for one reason or another seem to forget who is in charge of the joint and need a reminder. Then finally, there are the generally unwelcome individuals who happen to notice the wrong person, see the wrong thing, or ask the wrong question. Those unfortunate souls are typically scheduled for an intense little discussion here in the 'storage' room. This room

Roman frog sticker... and if you remember, he and the killer were all Italians... coincidence? No, business as usual.

Unfortunately for me, things aren't going well with my investigation at the moment. I think this little backroom get together is supposed to be more of a warning rather than an interrogation, so any questions would really be casual icebreakers before getting to the rough stuff.

I felt the sweaty goon in my face let go of my left lapel only long enough to grab a handful of my nicely starched and pressed Brooks Brothers dress shirt and my dark red Prada necktie. He jerked me up close and eye-stank me.

I don't like him. He smells of greasy french fries and Brute... or is that Hai Karate? Do they still make Hai Karate?

I don't think he likes me either.

Potato breath posed a question. "What's your name, asshole?"

Why lie when the truth will fit? Besides, I suspect this vomit sack's boss already figured out who I am and why I'm here.

"Becker."

"Becker who?

Just Becker."

"What are you doing here, asshole?"

Why did he bother asking my name if he was going to keep using my nickname?

"Mind if I have a cigarette?" I moved carefully,

like I was reaching for a pack of smokes in my inner jacket pocket. All that got me was a good shaking by the goon.

"I asked you a question, asshole!"

I guess that means no cigarette. So this definitely isn't a social occasion.

I began my counter-interrogation. "You're making a big mistake. Did Benelli tell you to do this?"

My favorite brand of shotgun was the only Italian name I could think of off the top of my head. Like I said, I suspected some Italian guy was part of the case so I threw a wide loop.

"I don't know no Benelli... I work for Conti, asshole. You're really stupid, you know that? How'd you ever get to be a private eye?" He pushed me away.

Thanks genius. Now I have a name.

I stalled with some on-the-fly ridiculous bullshit. "Look, man... Conti, Benelli, I don't know either of them...I'm waiting for my attorney so this conversation can meet its just and timely end. I have some rights in this country, mister." I indignantly straightened my suit. "Now, may I please have a cigarette?"

I think he smiled at my wit. Or maybe he's constipated... difficult to say with that face.

He yanked me in nose-to-nose, close enough so I could smell what had to be a combination of Hai Karate aftershave and Brut body spray, definitely unique. He's an innovator of fine essence, more or less.

"Not today, asshole. Maybe you got rights in this country but not in this casino, Becker. We're not cops." The goon's mouth twisted into a demonic grin. He now knew had me with his bear-trap-solid goon logic.

I admit, he had an excellent point. Maybe *he* was the brains of the group rather than the mouth-breather or the rapper. After all, he was doing most of the talking. And I appreciate him finally calling me Becker instead of asshole. It really feels like we are experiencing a breakthrough in our relationship. This might be a nice evening of warm fraternal bonding after all.

I countered his implied threat, "Yeah, you're right, you aren't cops... but *I* used to be a cop, a real cop, pal... and they taught us a pretty important lesson in cop training back in my day."

That got a full chuckle out of him. I guess he doesn't believe an old fat guy is going to cause much trouble... The tough talk coming out of a senior citizen sounded cute to him.

He growled back, gripping my lapels again and showing me his four or five randomly placed front teeth in a tight smile. "Oh yeah, what lesson was that, asshole?"

Again, with my nickname.

Instead of explaining, I demonstrated. A lot of people don't expect a cop to knee you in the nuts. I guess they haven't met all the cops, especially the old retired ones. We were able to live long enough to become old and retired cops for a reason. We don't hesitate to knee people in the nuts when the situation calls for it.

The blow felt like I smashed a bag of grapes.

His wandering eye converged with the normal one in a crossed configuration.

I windmilled my right arm around, coming up under and then across his elbows, stripping his grubby fingers from my clothes. Setting my hips, I delivered a two-hand power shove to his chest, creating some distance between us, followed by a full-power Lou Groza style kick to the crotch with enough juice on it to land a fifty-yard field goal.

I think those two solid shots to the gonads got him believing in Jesus again. Tough love works.

He grunted and collapsed.

He might have crapped his pants.

An essence more overpowering than his aftershave wafted through the air.

Eww...Yeah, he did crap 'em.

Stupid guy number two couldn't figure out what just happened. Out of my peripheral vision, I noticed him just standing there with his mouth open, maybe a little wider now and more slack jawed than before. While he stood there processing what he just witnessed, I decided to give stupid guy number three, the failed rapper, a big fat knuckle burger to the snot locker with a left before returning my attention to number two again and awarding him a right uppercut to the chin and an left elbow to the side of the melon near his temple.

They both went down, not that I'm a great puncher, they just didn't foresee an old-timer still being fast with his hands. Unwisely, they kept their own hands down during our chat, so I was able to tag each of them with nice full-power face shots. They had overconfidence in their numbers and underestimated their opponent. Those errors in judgement handed me my opening. A higher quality muscle-head wouldn't make that mistake.

Eww... The failed rapper is making a gurgling noise. Man, that nose is really leaking blood. He should get that looked at.

I rolled the rapper onto his stomach so he didn't choke to death on his own blood. I'm a humanitarian. Also, I hate it when I get manslaughter charges filed against me.

I evaluated my work.

The main goon had crawled off to the corner of the room. He curled up in a fetal position, puking. He probably was wishing he wore his brown pants today. The other two were sprawled on the cold concrete floor twitching.

Nice.

I straightened my necktie and strolled out of the room onto the main floor of the Casino, fast walking to the closest exit.

I saw all I came to see. I heard all I needed to hear.

I got a name.

I confirmed I'm on the right track.

Perhaps I was wrong about one thing.

This might my happy place after all.

The Becker Residence, Lauderdale by the Sea

After parking my four-year-old XF Jaguar sedan in the garage next to the convertible, then making my way past the quarters of my house manager, Mister Worm, I beelined to my favorite recliner on the patio and flopped down. It was a bit cool for a Florida winter evening, so I didn't bother dressing down to my loungewear, I chilled in my suit and hat. I did loosen my tie, though.

The little scuffle left me more tired than I thought it would. I blame that old age thing. I retired from the police department so long ago that even the last batch of rookies I worked with were retired now too. But if you are a cop, a real cop, you will always be a cop... even if you get old.

I need a drink.

"Worm! Cocktail time!"

Within seconds, the skinny and somewhat unkempt Mister Worm, a former criminal turned butler, brought me a Bulleit whiskey on the rocks adorned with a Luxardo cherry and a splash of water. His uniform of a light blue polo shirt, dark blue shorts, and a captain's hat appeared clean and pressed. Worm is really shaping up. Although his hair still looks like it was cut by a raccoon with a hedge trimmer.

"Your beverage, sir," he said slowly and deliberately, attempting to minimize his twangy Eastern Kentucky accent.

"Beverage?"

The accent returned. "I've been watching professional butlers on YouTube, Becker. They call this shit a beverage."

In spite of my respect for his attempting to raise the household level of sophistication, some things I can't buy into. "Yeah, well… here we'll call it a cocktail. YouTube is for commies."

"I prefer to call it a cocktail too."

Mister Worm almost always agreed with me. Smart guy. Then suddenly he disagreed with me. "But I think it's the other one that is the commies."

"The other one what?"

I threw back my drink like a cowboy in a saloon while he elaborated.

"The other video thing, Becker. I can't remember the name of it but it's owned by the commies. Not the Russians, the other ones… I don't think the Russians are still commies… But…"

"Worm…" I interrupted.

"Yes?"

"I don't give a shit."

"Just saying."

He looked sad. I think he was showing off his knowledge of world affairs and I cut him off. If

I was capable of having feelings, I'd feel a little guilty about my impatience. But my drink is gone, and all bets are off.

"Forget it, Worm. Make another cocktail and we can try this again. And make yourself one."

That order made him smile. He disappeared back into the kitchen.

My hands were starting to ache from the punching session at the casino and I didn't feel like debating Worm about communism and computer videos. As you get older, arthritis tends to invite lingering pain in the aftermath of physical exertion. It also makes me a little cranky. I had guzzled, rather than sipped, my first cocktail, for medicinal purposes only, of course.

Pain hurts.

"Worm!" I shouted toward the sound of clinking ice.

"Yeah, boss," she shouted back as he was preparing drinks.

"What do we have for sore knuckles?"

I heard the freezer door open on the Wolf and Cove Sub-Zero.

He shouted back. "Frozen peas or frozen mixed veggies, which looks like it might have broccoli in it... I'll bring you the peas."

"Thanks."

Sometimes having an ex-hood on hand is better than having an in-house medic. A hood can patch you up *and* they can mix a quality cocktail.

I try to keep frozen peas and corn stocked for general injuries. A pack of slightly defrosted spinach is good for sore eyes or fat lips... it's an old cop trick. Every guy who ever worked night shift on patrol division knows it.

There was a slight breeze blowing in from the canal, lifting the scent of the marina, diesel oil, salt water, and dead fish, into the air. It was my favorite smell. Other than when a sexy woman wears that Jean Nate or whatever it's called. The essence of lavender and jasmine attached to a woman's skin makes me weak-kneed and silly. It's like hormonal kryptonite. The crazy gold-digger Jeanine Faraday wears it. I wondered if she was still in town or if she found a new mark and was partying in the Bahamas. I hoped she was out of town. She is highly skilled at distracting detectives trying to conduct investigations. Luckily, her notorious charms have no effect on me. I rarely think of her.

I spotted my reading glasses on the side table. Good. I leave readers tactically placed near every location at which I might sit down. Not that I need them.

I put the empty glass down with my left hand as I fished for my notebook with the right. The truth is, I didn't want this case. I'm mostly retired. But if I do decide to take a job, I'll do it right. Besides, this is for a brother officer, old Nicolo DeCarlo, a retired motorcycle cop turned magician who is employed at the casino. Before we reconnected on this case, I didn't know being a magician was a real job. I knew there were some tricks you could buy at a magic store to entertain kids at birthday parties, but it turns out, being a professional magician is a very serious gig. And Nicolo has a hot assistant, a lady named Sonechka who speaks with some slightly Russian sounding accent.

Nicolo, a guy who is a little younger than me with a flattop haircut and a face that makes you feel like you should hand him your license and registration, works at our local casino doing two shows a night and pulling down some serious cash, at least serious for him. He wasn't in my tax bracket yet. Financially speaking, I'm not the normal retired cop. I'm comfortable, a term wealthy people use.

I am grateful to be 'comfortable' financially, with the pile of trust fund money my late wife left me when she passed. Life was simple then. I worked at what was interesting and tried to stay off the radar. Then, my somewhat 'hobbyist' investigation company scored two huge unexpected financial windfalls the past year. I can't even figure out how much money I have. It's a lot.

Even though I am what some might call wealthy, I still think like a low-salaried cop, so when a guy is making two thousand a night doing magic tricks, it seems like serious cash. Apparently, old Nicolo is pretty good at prestidigitation.

I began the review of my notes as Mister Worm appeared carrying my second cocktail, and presumably his first, along with the bag of frozen peas.

"Anything else, Becker?" Worm asked as he placed it all on the table.

"Yeah, we have a client. Get Joan, Tiki, and Dourdhoff over here so I can brief all of you together. And I need a sandwich to wash down these drinks."

"Yes, sir." He looked at me like I might have said that wrong. Before Worm disappeared into the house, he lit the fire pit and turned on the hot tub. He must be clairvoyant.

While he made drinks, I reviewed my notes.

Note one, Nicolo's assistant's friend is missing. She works in his act once in a while and the three of them are close. Not romantically close, as far as I know, not judging. The girls are close, they might have some history. I need to look into what the extent of that history is. Nicolo is paying me five-hundred bucks to find her. I'd do it for free, but Nicolo doesn't like owing people, even friends, and I respect that. The payment was a token gesture. Fair enough.

Note two, Nicolo's assistant's friend is a cocktail waitress at the casino. She's also easy on the eyes according to the photo he gave me. I suppose in a way, Nicolo's assistant is the real client, but she doesn't know a retired cop turned private eye.

Nicolo does.

Note three, when Nicolo and I were uniform cops about a million years ago, he once backed me up at a fight in the housing projects that I was slowly not winning in a rapid manner. He saved my ass. I don't forget shit like that. We got history, so this job is getting done right.

Note four, Nicolo's assistant's friend, the hot waitress, was having a romantic relationship with one of the major investors at the casino. Again, not judging.

And last but not least, note five, this major investor, who was playing hide the salami with the missing waitress, was found burned to death in the trunk of a car in the Everglades. Typical mob suicide.

The whole dead guy in the trunk thing wasn't that unusual here in sunny Florida, but this story piqued my curiosity. Why was he barbecued? How did the woman get away? Or did someone take her? Was she even alive? And how does a magician rate two thousand a night? That right there is a pretty good trick.

My mind is starting to wander, I need more whiskey... for the arthritis.

Worm appeared with two more drinks and a tray of sandwiches. He handed me a fresh cocktail and placed the tray on the table beside my chair.

"Sit down, Worm. I need to run something by you."

"Sure, Becker," he murmured as he sat in the deck chair beside me.

"You having a sandwich, Worm?"

"Sure… I could eat." He snatched a sandwich off the tray. I don't know how he stays so skinny. He eats like a horse. Must be metabolism.

I grabbed one too and took a big bite of the cold turkey, lettuce, and tomato sandwich. Worm always 'drains' the tomato slices so they aren't all wet and slippery ruining the bread. He learned a lot of pretty good chef tricks during his years working through parole as a fry cook in diners. His BLTs are to die for.

I raised my glass, "To absent companions."

"Cheers, Becker."

'We each took a sip before I posed a question.

"Why does a woman disappear when a man gets whacked?"

"Easy, either she did it or she's next."

"Why does a wealthy investor in a casino get shoved in a car trunk and burned alive?"

Worm thought about this one before answering. "Because he's an asshole, everyone he knows is an asshole, and burning a guy alive in a car is the kind of thing assholes do to each other… and others."

"That makes sense. But why?"

"Send a message. Money. Jealousy. Revenge. Asshole activity… One of those probably."

Worm is like an encyclopedia of maggot science. I'm grateful to have him even though he is a reformed career criminal and ex-bagman.

"I agree. Now, I need to sort all of that out and find this girl."

The doorbell rang. Worm scrambled to answer, adjusting his uniform and shooting a quick blast of breath spray in his mouth as he jogged to the door, although it was probably my crew arriving.

Moments later, my crew waltzed in, entering like they lived here. Retired Beverly Hills Police Lieutenant Joan Vance strolled through the house and out onto my patio accompanied by my computer guru and former high-school classmate Dourdhoff Jenkins. Tagging along was my newest employee and former informant, Tiki Cha Cha. Tiki was a street-smart prostitute in a former life, but now the feisty little Filipina is a straight arrow and turned out to be a pretty good detective. Our professional relationship dates back to when I threw a man who beat her up off a hotel balcony. She'd been a loyal ally ever since. With Worm, they constitute the current core staff of Becker Investigations.

Joan, who manages the agency's day to day business operations now, left California to create a little distance from her on-again off-again boyfriend Joe Tucker, a retired cop and owner of a private investigation firm in Los Angeles. She wore black jeans, a black silk blouse, and a gray blazer that concealed the Forty-Four Auto Mag she was gifted by her grandfather, some old retired cop named Earby from Mobile. I don't think her grandpa was anyone to screw with, and neither is his granddaughter. Joan pulled off a cool, detached, feminine-but-tough look with style, natural beauty, and yeah... firepower.

Tiki, once a victim of a vicious human trafficking ring, was a tiny Filipina woman with extreme feminine physical attributes. I'm not sure how you say big boobs and built like a brick shithouse in these modern times without getting protestors on your porch, so I'll stick with feminine physical attributes. English is her second language and sometimes I suspect there is a third unknown language in there somewhere that Tiki uses when she gets excited and starts spouting off. After I helped her get out of the trafficking ring, and with the help of an insurance settlement she was awarded from a traffic accident involving a city bus, she has been living well, spending her time studying traditional Japanese martial arts mixed with some boxing lessons. So, she's a bit tougher than the average stick of dynamite now and about the same size. She was sporting a casual but professional look, at least by Florida standards, with a short dark blue skirt and a maroon spaghetti strap blouse. She might be subtle and subdued in appearance at the moment, but she's my go-to detective when I need a visual distraction. She can quickly switch from invisible to stunning with little effort using her deep wardrobe of club clothes and natural sex appeal.

Dourdhoff, a high school pal and life-long friend, is a mega-rich computer genius and inventor, who routinely makes a million bucks before lunch, then helps me out the rest of the day just because he wants to. In addition to his wealth Dourdhoff is highly respected in nerd circles. That electric-car spaceship guy has him on speed dial. The Saudi King once flew him over in a private jet to program all the TV remotes in his palace. Durd was overqualified for that one but he was paid with a full and complete set of the famed Dirty Dozen wrist watches from World War II in mint condition. As a fellow watch collector, I'd have done that job too, except I can't program my own remote let alone a hundred of them. He has some weird connections, and his patents probably bring in a million a week of passive income. Durd is a good friend to have.

Dourdhoff skulked to his chair adorned in black BDU pants, a V-neck black T-shirt and a black Sinatra-style dress hat. I spotted the Breguet Marine Hora Mundi on his wrist. That had to set him back about seventy grand. But that was pocket change to him. Yet, in spite of his exquisite taste in high horology, still he wears the cheapest high-top black knock-off tennis shoes money is barely necessary to buy. On the police department, in the old days, we used to call them Felony Flyers.

Worm took drink orders as we gathered around the fire pit to discuss business. The back of my home faces a canal off the intra-coastal. A small marina and boatyard are at the end of the canal on the other side of the condos next door. A few times a day, either a small boat or a big yacht cruises by and sometimes the police marine patrol would stop in for bathroom and snack breaks. Not a lot of cops retire rich, so I was a bit of a celebrity among the younger guys, even though I'm a disagreeable old bastard... or so they say... *they*, being everybody but cops. Cops respect a guy who hates everybody, has no friends, and doesn't trust anyone. It's a trait we all share or aspire to... a trait or a curse.... maybe, a blessing.

Worm returned with the next tray of drinks, interrupting my wandering thoughts, and we went to work.

Joan, as is her style, began by getting right to the point. "What's on your mind, Becker?"

Joan is very organized, professional, and highly focused. Most people consider that a commendable quality. I agree with them, but it still makes me nervous. I've always believed that police work, and now the private investigation business, is more of an art than a science, so rules and structure make me uncomfortable. But she evolved my agency from a part-time hobby to a thriving cash cow, so I won't complain.

"Do we have much going on right now at the shop, Joan?"

She looked at the ceiling, activating her analytical mode, before answering. "Just the usual auto-pilot stuff. There's a request for 'local knowledge' from a San Diego P.I. named Glume. She just needs some direction on operating around town for a security op on a heavy metal band... you know, 'who to trust' and 'where to go' kind of stuff. I'm meeting her for lunch to do a consultation... professional courtesy thing. Everything else we need to do is pretty much automated now. But FYI, I'll still need to hire an office assistant at some point."

I considered her information and made a suggestion. Sometimes my suggestions sound a lot like orders. "Call Tommy from Lauderdale down at the bar and hire him to join you at lunch. He can assist the San Diego lady while she's here if it's just for local contacts, hot issues, and some tour guide work. If we are extending professional courtesy, let's do it right. Tommy knows the street as well as anybody. I can't imagine anything going wrong. Hire whoever you want for the office. Cash flow isn't an issue, so get someone good."

"Got it." Joan tapped some notes into her phone.

Having cleared the board of day-to-day operations issues, I got down to the mission at hand.

"I know you all recall my mentioning a friend of mine, Nicolo DeCarlo," I began, before being immediately interrupted.

Joan grumbled, "No, Becker. I don't remember you mentioning your friend. You never talk about anything. Is this 'mentioning shit' something new you're doing?"

Tiki jumped in, "And when did you get a friend? You hate everybody, Becker. And everybody hate your guts right back!"

Her heavy Filipina accent and broken English comes back in a big way when she smells blood in the water. Tiki, along with being somewhat volatile, is a bit mercenary and ruthless. She fits right in with our team.

I reframed the statement. "Fine, there is a guy I know named Nicolo DeCarlo. He does magic."

Dourdhoff asked, "Like Houdini or are you talking about some new drug?" Dourdhoff loves specificity.

"He does regular magic, you know…. American magic tricks… he performs at the casino a couple of times a night."

"So Houdini, then," Dourdhoff stated smugly.

Tiki jumped in, "Who?"

Dourdhoff saw an opening to dash into full 'know-it-all' mode, which I find annoying even though he does sort of know it all. "Harry Houdini was a stage name for an internationally famous escape artist and magician named Erich Weisz, circa the early twentieth century. He famously said, 'What the eyes see and the ears hear, the mind believes.' His fame included acts of…"

I put my hand up. "We got it Durd." I groused, using Dourdhoff's nickname. In high school we used to call him Durd the Turd. He hated that. Just 'Durd' though, he finds acceptable.

Tiki was impressed with the story, "No, I want to hear more."

Joan put a hand on Tiki's shoulder, "Focus... otherwise we'll be here for hours."

Tiki nodded submissively to Joan, then gave Dourdhoff the 'telephone' hand gesture as she mouthed, *call me*.

I continued, "Nicolo has a..."

This time it was Worm interrupting.

"One time in Tijuana I saw a woman named Queenie Houdini star in a show. She would hide a whole..."

"JUST NO!" I scolded him sharply with a scowl and a finger point before he went any further, not that any of us were politically correct but... just, no.

Worm was unfazed. "Well, it was worth the five bucks to see."

I heard Tiki snicker.

I gave him a death glare, then her a death glare, and then went into distraction mode. "Worm, refresh everyone's drinks please."

"I just..."

I gave him an even more malicious squint that suggested I'd just as soon kill him as look at him.

He skittered away towards the kitchen. Message received.

Everyone calmed down.

In a moment Worm returned with more drinks.

I might need to send everyone home in ride-shares tonight.

I continued with my briefing. "Okay, Nicolo was a cop. Now he has a magician gig at the casino. His assistant is a lady with an interesting eastern European accent. Her friend is missing."

I passed my notes to Dourdhoff and he tapped them into his computer then distributed them to everyone's phone using computer wizardry bullshit stuff.

Joan frowned. "So, a simple missing person case requires a team meeting? Just give the case to me. I'll go round her up," she said confidently.

"The missing girl was having a fling with their boss... a big money man."

"So?"

"He was found burned up in the trunk of his car."

"That will kill you," Tiki observed, causing me to momentarily miss the good old days when I worked alone.

"Yes, Tiki. It certainly will do that," I confirmed.

She nodded enthusiastically as if we both just agreed on a formula for the Grand Unification Theory of physics.

Dourdhoff was now interested, "Mob?"

I frowned, "Maybe. All I know is I went into the casino to ask a few questions when the in-house goon squad tried to put the bag on me."

Joan snapped from attentively listening to an expression of deep concern. She put her hand on the back of mine and squeezed it to make sure she had my complete attention. "Becker, you should have called me to go along."

She's becoming a bit of a mother hen. I admit that I'm old, but I'm not feeble. Nevertheless, the concern is appreciated.

"It's fine. I just wanted to find out if simply asking about this subject would get the attention of at least one of the owners. No one other than an owner has the juice to send security goons to jack up someone who isn't cheating at gambling or causing a disturbance. Especially if that someone is a licensed P.I."

"Is the girl dead?" Joan asked coldly as she slowly withdrew her hand. Her years in robbery/homicide led her to be blunt in this type of situation. Cops look at homicide like a dentist looks at a cavity. You just drill it out it, fill it, and get paid. The pain it might cause is something you simply accept because it's the only way to make it right.

"Maybe," I replied. "Worm had some good perspective on it. He thinks if she isn't dead then she's on the run. Not saying she won't be dead soon either way. Time is an issue. We need to get on this shit show chop-chop."

"What's her name?" Tiki asked. Tiki didn't bother reading the notes from her phone that

Dourdhoff sent her. Tiki brings high-level street sense and cunning to the team, old school stuff. I respect that. Technology appreciation though, not so much for Tiki... like me.

I answered. "Monica Brand... at least that's the name she is using now. I haven't pulled a file up on..."

Dourdhoff, who had been banging away on his keyboard responded, "Monica Brand, AKA Mona Boyle, AKA Misty Masters, which is I assume is some sort of a professional moniker. Her last known address is an apartment in Wilton Manors."

"Is she gay?" I asked, based on the neighborhood demographics.

Tiki interjected with a slight hint of scolding in her tone, "Lot of girls like living there. It's safer and gay men are polite and very sweet eye-candy. Not like you guys." She waved a finger at me, Durd, and Worm. You are all just rude knuckle-dragging hairy cavemen. Girls don't feel safe around you."

Worm shined one of his rare smiles, "Thank you, Tiki. I appreciate that."

Tiki appeared confused, but somehow I understood how he perceived being called a knuckle-dragging cave man as being a compliment. I spend too much time with Worm. Being able to read his thought process is unnerving.

I grumbled. "Tiki, an investigator has to ask

difficult questions bluntly. Nothing was meant to demean anyone, and I don't have time to make a multiple choice question. And by the way, who is more blunt than you, lady?"

Tiki pouted. She pouts a lot. It is her best manipulation tool. Her pout is adorable. Luckily it doesn't affect me in any way.

I think I made my point, although I'm not sure what my point was, so I continued, "We need the police reports on the dead guy, I need to know any mob connections he might have. I need to have her home checked and her neighbors interviewed." I realized I was spouting orders like I did with my detectives on the police department. I miss that. Interestingly, I think my team likes being addressed that way.

"Joan, see if you can find one of her friends at the casino. Tiki, run cover for her but stay invisible. We might need you to be a fresh face later."

"No problem boss."

"Dourdhoff, take Worm. You two go get an eye on her last known address. See if there is any activity. Use two cars."

Dourdhoff smiled, "I'll take my van and put up one of the drones. I can cover the immediate area with tech. Worm can run down anything mobile on the ground."

Worm gave a thumbs up.

I liked that plan. "Smart... go for it."

"You got it boss," Dourdhoff said with a little

salute.

It was time to let them do their thing. I addressed the whole group before we split up. "Okay, hit the streets. I'll catch a cat nap and a shower. Oh, Durd... send me the dead guy's address. I'll go sit on it for a while after I get up."

"Sounds good, boss," Worm said. "I'll make everyone a care package of snacks and drinks before we go."

Good old Worm. The best, and only, butler I ever had.

I noticed no one touched the last couple of rounds of cocktails and Worm had already distributed cups of coffee around the room. They were good to go.

I gave a slow wave as I walked upstairs to my room. Fighting makes me tired. They all knew what to do. This was probably just some jealous boyfriend, scared girl on the run thing that we would wrap up in forty-eight hours at the most.

I'd change into a swimsuit, do a half an hour in the spa to loosen up the joints, not that I was stiff and sore from the fight at all, and then get some sleep.

With a billionaire nerd, a reformed crook, a former California cop recovering from a bad relationship, and an ex-hooker on the job, all helping a retired detective who old enough to collect social security, how could anything go wrong?

CHAPTER 2 - THE GIRL

The alarm clock startled me awake after a forty-five-minute power nap. I showered and dressed in a plain black suit with a linen Brooks Brothers dress shirt and black and gray striped silk tie. I slipped my Cartier Santos on my wrist. In spite of my healthy collection of nice watches, I was having a difficult time wearing anything else. All my wrist time was committed to the Santos or occasionally my Casio Duro when I was out working on the boat. All my other watches were presently 'safe queens' locked up until I felt the need for a change.

I tossed my black Goorin Nighthawk dress hat on my head and wandered downstairs. It was time to go to work.

I noticed an insulated bag of food and two thermos bottles on the table waiting for me. One thermos was marked coffee and the other was labeled tea, which is our code for Honey Whiskey which hits the spot on a long cold surveillance. Good old Worm.

Whenever the Iguanas start dropping out of trees unconscious, it's cold enough for surveillance whiskey.

It's a Florida thing.

I checked my phone. There was an address

and maps marking the location of the dead guy's house, plus Dourdhoff added some more history on the guy. I read the report. The home of 'Mister Burned Up in the Trunk' might be a good hide-out for the girl. They wouldn't be looking for her there.

I turned onto Commercial Boulevard and headed for his place in Pompano Beach. I'd go down the Federal Highway and take a shortcut I knew. In ten minutes, I was sitting on a side street with an eye on the house.

Surveillance is a game of blending in and covertly observing the target person or location in question. It can be mobile or stationary. Tonight it was stationary. My Jaguar looked right for the neighborhood, so I parked on the property line between two estates so if either home noticed me they would shrug it off as someone visiting their neighbors. Burglars and home invaders don't usually drive Jaguars. The XF Jag could even pass for a luxury car service vehicle, something one or two passengers might request rather than a limo.

I was good. I was invisible in this upscale neighborhood.

I relaxed and watched. I didn't really expect to see anything. The others hadn't reported any activity either.

I opened the window a crack. The thick moist essence of jungle air slipped through the opening. These upscale neighborhoods with the dense landscaping and canal waterfronts all have that unique natural Florida scent of bugs, flowers, marine diesel, and swamp rot. I like it.

The report Durd sent me provided more questions than answers. The dead man's name, according to the immediately available public information resources, was Joseph Luca. The papers said he was an investor and capitalist who moved to Florida two years ago. There wasn't any public information on him preceding the move. The picture looked a lot like a guy who was auditioning for the lead hood in a gangster picture. Talk about stereotypes. But here's the thing about stereotypes... they are usually based on reality. Stereotypes come from a basic survival instinct engrained in humans since back in the dinosaur days and maybe before. It's human nature to take in a lot of data and quickly generalize it in order to sort potential threats from safe situations. Experienced cops have developed it to a super-power level. They can read a life story at a glance with a ninety-seven percent accuracy. I'm not saying all that is pure science, but nobody is telling me I'm wrong either.

Most mobsters have some mobster charisma going on, and it appears the late Mister Luca was no exception. So, this hit might be a mob thing. I don't care about the 'mob thing' part and I don't care about Mister Luca. I only want to find the lost girl. According to Sonechka, Nicolo's assistant, our missing woman was in her early forties. She became close with Sonechka at work, like a big sister. She reportedly fell in love with this hood because of his charm and money, but mostly the money. She wanted to be the girlfriend or wife of a successful man, and from what I was told, even a successful hood would do. Not necessarily a bad game plan. One can love a rich jerk just as much as one can love a poor jerk, I suspect.

The stereotype gangster, Mister Luca, was a mystery man and the missing woman seemed to be an obvious stereotype gold-digger. But in this game, we never assume anything. We investigate and confirm or clear information. People are too random to trust a stereotype with your life.

After an hour or so of drinking coffee and contemplating the puzzles of life, I started looking for a place to pee. I'm old and I pee too damn much.

I spotted a tall hedge by a cul-de-sac that I thought might work when a stupid Prius rolled up to the target house. It was black like my Jaguar and had a ride-share emblem in the window. It stopped and a woman, who might be my girl, bailed out and ran to the house. The car waited.

I hate Priuses, but not for the reason you think. I don't care if people drive electric cars as long as I never have to. But when I'm on surveillance, I can't hear them roll up on me.

I fired up the Jag and wheeled in behind him. I could see the driver rubber-necking, wondering what was up.

I hopped out and approached the driver window

like a traffic cop. I flashed my old retirement badge quickly in his face and just as quickly stuffed it back in my pocket. "Beat it pal. You are transporting a fugitive. Leave now and I'll just give you a warning."

I came on strong enough that he burned rubber out of there like he had to pee too. Lucky bastard. I have to hold it.

I moved my car up to where his was parked then got out with my thermos and hid by a property line fence. If she asked him to wait, then she would be coming out quickly.

I waited.

It was taking longer than I thought it would.

I opened the thermos out of habit.

A cup of coffee later, I needed to pee even more. Sometimes I get it in my head that drinking a cup of coffee when I need to pee will take my mind off of peeing. So far, this has never proven true, but I still do it. I might be my own worst enemy. People have told me that before but I never believed them... maybe they were on to something. I screwed the cup/lid back on the thermos and waited.

I squirmed.

It was getting serious.

Dammit.

Moments later, I see a red-haired woman with big knockers and long shapely legs come dashing out of the estate carrying a briefcase. She doesn't seem to know cars, so she started to get into the back of my Jag. I suspected there might be a chance of that happening. I was counting on it.

I tiptoed up behind her and choked her out.

It was easy, she went night-night real quick.

I know, choking a woman out on a dark street seems rude, but do remember the part about me needing to go pee? She lingered around the house way too long, so really, it's her fault, not mine.

I tossed her limp body in the trunk, taking the briefcase with me front up front in case there was a gun in it. I dropped the thermos into the cup holder as I did a Parnelli Jones to my unofficial public restroom, a dumpster in a nearby dark parking lot behind a local strip mall where I have peed during other cases in this neighborhood.

I barely made it to behind the dumpster in time.

Frequent pee breaks are the thing I hate the most about getting older. But I don't hate it enough to stop guzzling coffee. I guess this is simply another one of life's mysteries we won't solve tonight.

Ahhhhh….

That's better.

I'm thinking more clearly now. Maybe I shouldn't have choked her out. In retrospect, it was pretty harsh. Oh well… I'm sure she'll understand.

Bladder relieved and trousers secured, I lifted her out of the trunk, stood her up, and gave her a couple of gentle slaps to wake her up, in a professional way.

She startled into consciousness.

The fear was burning in her wide blue eyes. She expected to be murdered. In violent defiance, she tried to jerk away from me, but I'm a big son of a bitch and held her in place by her arm. She was dressed in revealing night club clothes, obviously high quality designer rags, but I don't recognize which brand, so perhaps they are bespoke. However, she'd been wearing them for over the past twenty-four hours while she's been on the run. The outfit was wrinkled and stained, and she smelled of Dior J'adore Eau de Parfum, gin, and woman sweat. She wanted to fight but didn't know how. The woman was on the brink of a panic breakdown.

I spoke softly, trying to defuse this stick of emotional dynamite. "Sonechka sent me. I'm a friend of Nicolo."

"Sonechka?" she whispered, calming slightly. "You know Nicolo?"

"Yes, I'm here to help. Sonechka was worried when you disappeared. They hired me to find you and get you to safety. My name is Becker."

"Becker who?"

"Just Becker."

She calmed down a bit, slightly relaxing but still on edge.

She blinked her way through some thoughts before speaking. "Wait, are you Nicolo's friend he calls the goon private eye? You two were cops together?"

I snickered, "Yeah, he might have called me that. I prefer to think of myself as a professional problem solver."

I let her go and shook a Lucky Strike out of the pack I keep in my inside jacket pocket and offered it to her. She nodded and took it. I touched the tip with the flame of my Zippo before lighting one for myself. I'm old enough to remember when having a cigarette with someone meant something.

"Why did you choke me out?" she snarled.

I blew a smoke cloud out of the corner of my mouth. "I had to pee."

"Oh…" She thought about it for a moment while she took a drag on her smoke. "Makes sense."

"Yeah, sorry." I was developing some new found respect for this woman. She has a firm grasp on the concept of cause and effect. I took a long drag on my Lucky.

I blew a malformed smoke ring into the thick Florida night air, then began tugging the information thread. "What's going on?"

She got to the point without asking me for any clarification, as if she expected this conversation was already in the cards for her.

"Did you read what they did to Luca? It was in the papers."

She took another puff on the cigarette.

"I got away."

She blew a pretty good smoke ring of her own. Maybe better than mine. But it's not a contest.

The woman was chatting freely now, yet her body was tense. Her posture was tight and angular. She was still acutely defensive. I could see sweat beads running down her cleavage, not that I was looking.

Oh my, are those freckles?

Focus!

But those freckles are sexy as hell…

FOCUS!

I answered her. "Yeah, I heard about it. Tough way to go." I wasn't sure how to respond, so I didn't offer any condolences. If she loved the guy she'd be heartbroken. If she loved his money she'd be pragmatic. I'd wait and see before saying much.

She flipped an ash of her cigarette. "I know what you're thinking. Stupid broad plays with mobster… cheesy gold-digger. But I did care for him a little, before I found out what he was really like… he was evil, Becker…"

So, it was both. She was a gold-digger but one with feelings for the guy… more or less. Women are complicated. They are the only mammal or reptile… depending on the woman, on the planet that can love and hate, reject and want, or be happy and sad at the same time. Five of them can talk at once and still hear what all the other ones are saying. They're like some kind of scary aliens… with sex appeal… at least some most of them are that way. I haven't met all of them yet.

"Evil?" I tried the active listening thing where I repeat her last word.

"Yeah, he was a murderer and a criminal. Mob man. He was just using me."

"And?" I asked.

"And now I'm in trouble." She made a sniffle sound.

That was an understatement.

I acknowledged the obvious. "It doesn't take a detective to figure that out, Miss…"

I knew her name, but I wanted to know if she'd lie about it.

She answered. "Monica. Monica Brand."

"Is that your real name?"

"It is now," she answered with a dead-eyed stare.

Fair enough. She's street smart, pragmatic, and a little tougher than her exterior would suggest.

I pressed her further. "So what kind of trouble are we talking about, Monica?"

"Big trouble. I know too much."

"Too much about what?"

"Luca… I know who killed him and I know why. I know the name of the main guy."

"And…"

"I think they're going to kill me for knowing it."

"And…"

"They will kill anyone they think I might have told. That means Nicolo and Sonechka…

They don't really know anything, but that doesn't matter... Now you're in danger too, Becker."

Then a thought crossed my mind, Nicolo and Sonechka... Joan and Tiki. They were all at the casino... and yeah, someone bad could easily conclude that they knew too much too. This is escalating fast.

Shit.

I escorted her to the passenger side and put her in the Jaguar. "Let's go."

I called Joan as we fought our way through traffic. She picked up right away.

"Yeah, Becker," she answered with loud casino noise in the background. I could visualize her with the phone pressed against her head with a finger in her opposite ear

I ran it down fast. "I got the girl. But the guys who whacked Luca are going to erase the information bloodline. Nicolo and Sonechka are targets. You could be collateral damage."

"Yay!" She said flatly. Usually that word is used a bit more gleefully in conversation. But cops are sarcastic. Retired cops are very sarcastic. Joan is a very sarcastic retired cop with a wide streak of insubordination in her...whatever... it runs in the blood... police genetics.

I spouted off some orders. "We're on our way to the safe house. Pick up the magician and his girl then meet us there. Let Durd and Worm know too. We'll figure this shit out over there."

"Sounds good." She disconnected the call.

I turned my attention to Monica. "Why didn't you warn your friends?" I spit the words out a bit more harshly than I intended to, but I was incensed at her and the situation we were now in. Nicolo was trying to help her, yet she left him and Sonechka hanging with targets on their backs.

Monica, unfazed by the fire in my tone, explained, "I couldn't risk it in case they don't know who they are my friends yet. I only used the phone for the ride-share, I didn't have a choice on that... But I didn't want to use it to make a call. I think these bastards might have my phone hacked. I went to Luca's place to get a burner phone and cash. He keeps both in his home office."

"Show me."

Monica handed me what appeared to be a standard burner. She also flashed a wad of cash. Yeah, she just burgled her dead boyfriend's house.

Shit happens.

I gave the burner back to her.

"We're going to a safe house I keep in Coral Gables. The team will meet us there. Then we sort out our options."

I saw a flash of light to the south.

Fireworks?

She shrugged.

My phone rang. It was Vance. She was amped up, not a good sign coming from her.

"Car bomb, Becker! We had a detonation."

"What?"

Car bomb in the parking lot."

"Who?"

"Nicolo's girl. She's gone."

I yelled into the phone, "Get the hell out of there, Vance."

"Copy that. We have Nicolo with us. Moving!"

I started bending some traffic laws and watching more closely for tails. So far, it seemed like we were okay, but I wasn't wasting any time getting Monica to the safe house.

"What?" Monica asked, a hint of fear appeared in her eyes.

"They killed Sonechka. Car bomb."

The previously stoic Monica's face quivered, then she broke down into flowing tears and snot... It looked sincere. When boogers come, you know they might be crying for real.

Monica did the 'talking and bawling at the same time thing,' chopping words and sucking air. "This is all my fault. I got my best friend killed."

"Yeah, you did." Comforting others is not my best skill. But maybe my approach is what she needed. I handed her my spare handkerchief. I keep two, one for show and one for blow.

Monica quickly regained control and wiped her face on her forearm. Something came over her. She changed. The devastated young woman was suddenly replaced with a cold and calculating jungle animal. Rage overcame grief and guilt.

Some people are like that... I'm like that.

Her upper lip curled into a determined snarl. "We're making them pay, Becker."

"Maybe you are making them pay, not me. I'm only here to save your ass."

"Then I'll hire you."

"With what?"

"I know where Luca kept a storage locker full of untraceable cash. I'll get your fee from there."

Now, I'm a rich man by most people's standards, and I don't need cash, especially mob cash, and all the drama that comes with them hunting for you for eternity. But the idea of packing a big fat kielbasa up the cartel's keister sounded like a good time to me. I can put the money to better use than they will. Still, the whole 'warehouse full of cash' thing didn't ring entirely true... but it rang loud enough to get my attention.

"Fine. But if that cash is crime proceeds, it gets turned over to the cops. I have a buddy I can call who does RICO seizures. You can grab enough to pay me my standard fee first though."

I'm rich, but I'm not stupid. I have payrolls to make.

"What do you get for this kind of job?" she asked.

So, Monica was a bit thrifty. I wonder if the flowing red hair indicated some Scottish blood in her veins.

"Ten thousand a week, three weeks minimum."

I lied. I don't have a set fee. Or maybe I do now, I'll have to ask Joan. She handles the business side of the operation. I just did this kind of work out of boredom before she came on board. People used to tell me how much they had to spend, and I'd decide if the job was worth the effort.

Monica continued, "And… we take out whoever killed my friend."

"I owe Nicolo that much. Agreed then?"

"Done."

Business negotiations usually go smoothest when you are dividing up someone else's money and killing people you were going to kill anyway.

Did I say kill? I meant, turn over to the rightful authorities… more or less.

We got down to the brass tacks of this thing. "Tell me the ten-cent version of this, Monica. What's going on?"

"Luca was an evil piece of shit, but he was an angel compared to these new psychos."

"What psychos?"

"The Mexican cartels."

"Seriously?" What were they doing in the casino business, I wondered.

I had bumped titties with the Columbian cartel bosses here in South Florida before. The Columbians are as much of a part of Florida culture as alligators and mullets. I didn't realize the border bandits had their eye on our little piece of paradise as well.

"Yeah, they are investing heavily in expanding money laundering and political influence for the cartel distribution structure. The number one money laundering opportunities are in the casinos... but it's not just casinos, they are hitting every cash business and company in Southeast Florida right now. I don't know about the rest of the country, but this is pretty bad.

"Mexican nationals?"

"Cartel isn't just local border gangs and corrupt government anymore. They have Chinese, Arab, and Russian guys too... They are international."

"Yeah, that's kind of bad. How do you know all this?"

"Pillow talk. Luca talked too much, that's why he was murdered first. He was a macho asshole and thought he could handle these guys... they showed him different."

"That's some serious pillow talk, lady. You seem to understand the business pretty well for a... girlfriend."

That comment lit her up. The fire in her eyes flared up as hot as her flowing red hair.

"You don't know me, Becker... I'm not sure you want to," she snarled.

I took a second or two of silence to process that advice. Maybe I underestimated this woman.

"You're right, maybe I don't." I growled back.

Some topics are best left unknown, especially if there is the possibility of formal depositions and indictments later. Her history, for now, was one of those topics. I switched back to the original line of questioning, completely ignoring her sexy legs and wholesome rack. They had no effect on me. I wasn't distracted by them at all. I barely thought about those cute cleavage freckles either.

Her story drove another question. I asked, "What do you mean when you said they 'killed him first?'"

"The cartel is going to whack anyone who is in their way and any outsider who knows their business. No buyouts and no negotiations. It won't be pretty."

"How do you know that."

"I heard them tormenting him on a phone call. Luca always used the speaker phone at home."

"So, were you there when they put the bag on him?" I asked.

"Yeah, they took him down at a drug store parking lot. He dropped me off to pick up a prescription, when I came out, I saw three carloads of them drag him out of the Bentley, kick his ass, shove him in the back seat of one of their cars, and drive off. One of them came after me but I ran out the back door of the pharmacy and kept running. I never looked back."

I frowned. "Not ideal for your boyfriend."

She frowned too. "Yeah, it's not."

We drove in silence for a few minutes. She gave me the internationally recognized hand sign for 'let me bum another cigarette...' The V-fingers and pouty lips. I shook one out of the pack for her. While she snatched it up, I started to fish in my pocket for my lighter. I was too slow, she torched it with her own lighter. It looked gold, maybe a Dupont. Probably a gift from her late boyfriend, mister dead guy.

She cracked the window and blew some smoke out into the night air. "Becker, we might be screwed."

"That's nothing new, Miss Brand. But I promise you, I'll get it sorted out and we'll find who killed your friend.

"I'm good with that. Afterwards I want to get as far away from this place as I can get."

"That's up to you, Monica. But getting out of Dodge City and staying out would be the smart move. The cartels have a long memory."

"Yeah, well, so do I, Becker. So do I."

CHAPTER 3 - THE PROMISE

My one-word-text, *'arrived,'* let Vance know we were rolling up.

"There might be people around, slouch down in the seat. I don't want anyone to see you."

She complied without a word.

I punched the code into the complex entrance gate and wheeled a hard left onto the drive where the condominium was located. Joan had opened the private garage door for me at our safe house. I wheeled in, got out, and hit the close button before I let Monica step out of the car. A quick glance down the street confirmed there wasn't a tail. We were as safe as we were going to be for time being.

The whole crew was on site now, including the clients, waiting in the dining room where we then gathered around the table. I say clients in the plural since I consider Monica a client now too, in addition to Nicolo and Sonechka... Sonechka our deceased client. I felt terrible, Nicolo was still in shock. Who wouldn't be... your girl hops into your car and gets blown to bits.

I walked into a quiet room. Joan and Tiki were on one side, Durd and Worm sat at the table across from Nicolo who was still in his magician costume with his red-lined black cape and fez. I put my hand on Nicolo's shoulder. "Sorry, brother... we didn't see that coming."

His eyes were moist. He looked up and nodded, but didn't speak. He needed some time. Monica scooted in beside him and put her arms around him, saying nothing, but expressing everything. In spite of what they say, sharing a loss, doesn't make it much lighter than just suffering alone. Then I noticed Monica putting her hand on his thigh and hugging him with the other arm. She hugged him a *long* time, almost intimately. Nicolo didn't respond.

Everyone processes grief differently.

"I need a drink." I torched a smoke and walked into one of the back rooms to think. I wasn't ready to start a case briefing. I had to get my thoughts straight.

Worm, in his off-duty attire of jeans, a black t-shirt, and a ball cap, followed me a minute later with a scotch and water on the rocks. I think he held the water, which is how I like it.

Worm whispered, "He's not in good shape, Becker."

"Nicolo?"

"Yeah."

"I know. But he's tough. Give him a few minutes."

Worm nodded and left. I finished my drink and cigarette then came back in to join the others. I still didn't know what I was going to say or do, but I was going to do something, anything... and see where it goes.

I'll just wing it. Get the ball rolling. Make something happen.

I went on autopilot, like the old days, letting my intuition guide me on what to do or say first. Plans are for pussies.

I found myself standing in front of my old police department buddy, giving him an option.

"Nicolo, we're going to debrief. It won't be pretty. Do you want to wait in the other room... take a break?"

He looked up at me. His eyes were red and his face drawn tight as an overinflated tire... "I might be retired Becker, but I'm still a cop. When Sammy got it, did we need to go lay down in the other room or did we hunt down the animal responsible? I'm in. Don't worry about me. I'm okay. I'll deal with the loss when the job is done."

I gave him a long look into the eyes. They say the eyes are the window to the soul, but they are also hard-wired into the brain. I heard some guy on television say they were part of the brain. I don't know if that is true. But a long look in the eyes will tell you what you need to know, chemical influence, anger, psychosis, sorrow... the eyes will reveal the truth about everyone but a psychopath, and Nicolo is not one of those. Nicolo is a straight shooter and we share the same old school values, you jerk him around, he's going to jerk you around... and you decide how far it goes. No limits.

"Fair enough, you're in..." I gave everyone else the eye. "We're going through this piece by piece. Don't pull any punches or sandpaper the facts. He can take it. Nicolo is my friend and our client. We owe it to him to do this right and be as specific as possible. Even graphic details... We're cleaning up this mess. Sonechka is getting payback." I looked at Vance. She knows what happens when a cop's loved ones get messed with. She squared her jaw and gave me a slight nod. Joan might look abundantly hot, but she's fully capable of being every bit of a violent and merciless vigilante as I am. Her years working on the L.A. County Organized Crime Task Force forged her into that. She'd done three years in that role before being shot by a gang member operating on the orders of her own boss. Her partner died at the scene. She lived through it and got her revenge... it wasn't pretty. I suspect Joan might have murdered every maggot involved in that atrocity. Case closed. Not judging... she's my kind of people, I get it.

When it comes to payback, the rest of the team is on board too. Worm and Tiki would do whatever the hell I told them to do and Dourdhoff loves this shit for some reason. Monica and Nicolo were in it for the revenge, so I'm predicting this will be a unanimous decision.

"We're going to take down whoever is responsible. They'll come back at us hard. If you want out, no hard feelings."

Dourdhoff was first, "Yeah, I'm in." He didn't bother looking up from his computer keyboard. He was already nerding the shit out of the case.

Tiki added, "Let's finish this boss, it could have been Tiki in that car bombing... Tiki wants to get pay back."

Since when did she start talking about herself in the third person?

Worm gave me a thumbs up.

Monica spoke, "She was my friend. If we don't finish it, we'll all share the same fate."

Nicolo hung his head and added his obviously heartfelt appreciation, "Thank you. Thank you all." His eyes might have watered had he not been a motorcycle cop. I think they have their tear ducts removed during training.

I put a hand on his shoulder, "Thank us when we wrap it up. This could be a little bigger than what we're used to... no guarantees any of us get through this alive."

Monica added, "It's guaranteed we'll all be dead if we don't stop them."

"Fair enough. Joan, you start."

My partner and business manager began, "Tiki and I set up cover on Nicolo and Sonechka like you told us... Nothing unusual was going on. I followed Nicolo to the backstage area so he could get his gear bag while Sonechka went to valet to get their car."

Tiki picked it up from there. "I shadowed

Sonechka to the car from a short distance. The valet brought it around and let her in the passenger side. I waited at the casino doors. Some drunk guy from out of town started a disturbance at the valet stand, so her valet ran over to help. That's when the car blew up. It knocked me on my ass."

"Are you okay?" Dourdhoff asked.

"Tiki fine... not first time with car bomb."

I snorted, reminiscing on the old Southeast Florida vice war back when I was a young cop. Yeah, there was a few car bombs and drive-by shootings every month for a while...Man, that was a fun time to be a police officer. But maybe Tiki doesn't remember it like I did.

"What happened next, Tiki?" I asked.

"Big fire... No hope for Sonechka. I found Joan and Nicolo...we ran for it."

I felt like we were missing something. But what?

"Dourdhoff, do you have anything yet?"

"Not much... the car burned at an unusually high temperature... nothing left."

Nicolo blanched, suppressing a sob... or maybe it was just a cough... I'll call it a cough... poor bastard.

I gave some orders, "From this point on, we work in pairs. Nicolo, you're partnered with Durd. Do you have a weapon?"

"Just a Glock 26."

"That won't be enough. Durd, can you get him a

G17 and a shotgun?"

"No problem."

"Are we going to war, Becker?" Monica asked.

"No, we're ending one."

Half an hour later I was sitting with a bottle on the small deck of the back bedroom, patching together a plan while the crew did research and continued analyzing the night's happenings.

I could hear them in the dining room bickering and making cases for their theories... each the other tearing their ideas to shreds... which is good. But we need a plan. As the most experienced detective, I already have one in progress. Part one of my plan, pour a glass of Bulleit Whiskey and drink it while I thought through the case. Bulleit has some secret ingredient that makes me think better. I took a big sip.

I'm feeling smarter already.

I still don't know anything though.

Smart might be overrated.

Cunning... Yeah, cunning is what we need.

Luckily, Bulleit does that too.

I'm still in the weeds on this. What we know so far is one thing... someone is killing everybody connected to Monica, that much seems obvious... but are we getting caught up in the fast moving events or are we thinking this through like professionals? What was obvious about any of this, really? Every angle had an angle.

It would be ideal to turn the entire case over to the cops while we get out of the country for an extended vacation. But we really didn't have much to give the cops... there was the rub. We believed we were on a kill list, but there was no hard evidence of the list actually existing. Really, the only person who was clearly in danger now was Monica. But then, why did they kill Sonechka? Was she the target? The real target? We can't even prove the dead guy in the car trunk and Sonechka's car bomb death were related. It all just *seems* related.

Obvious? No... obvious shouldn't even be a real word. Nothing is ever as it seems.

For some reason, my thoughts drifted to the freckles on Monica's cleavage. I'm not having carnal thoughts about them, I'm a professional. But it's important to verify that the freckles are not a relevant part of the case.

And what about the casino grab? We need to know more about that... nothing says it has to be the cartel. It might be other rivals in the criminal world. A few overheard phone conversations don't mean anything... those can be misinterpreted, misunderstood, or flatly mistaken.

Yeah, we know Jack shit... and Jack just got on the bus to Orlando with his mouse hat while all the shit stayed behind with us.

These kinds of circumstances are exactly why I preferred the fugitive detail and habitual offender surveillance team when I was a cop.

Jump teams were where it was at. Solving cases with investigations, witnesses, and evidence was bullshit. Catching them in the act of committing an armed robbery and just smoking the bastards was much cleaner. Justice is a dish best served with a punch below the belt and a kick in the teeth, or even a bullet in the guts... offender's choice.

Thinking, deducing, and sorting clues isn't nearly as much fun.

I couldn't come up with any answers... so, we'd need some names. We needed to talk to people who might know the skinny about what was up. The only name I had was the one the goons at the casino inadvertently gave up... Conti.

How did I forget about Conti?

Duh... I need a tête-à-tête with Conti. Maybe some things *are* obvious.

"Durd!" I yelled from the back room.

A second later he came scurrying in. "What's up?"

"Did you do a work up on Conti?"

"Yeah... Gino Conti, he has distant mob relations but he's just a guy... a guy who runs a casino... not a nice guy, but not a gangster."

"Shit."

"Yeah... So, why did you get the welcoming committee when you went there? Conti is in charge of the joint for all intents and purposes now that Luca is dead. Why would he have his guys rough you up?"

"They didn't rough me up, we just talked."

"Yeah, so why did that happen then?"

"I guess I can ask him.

"I'll go with you."

"No… everybody else needs to stay here until we have some idea of what we are into."

"You just told us all to work in pairs… what about you?"

"I'm special. I know what I'm doing."

Dourdhoff gave me the silent dead eye stare… the silent dead eye stare is worse than stink eye… it projects shame and revulsion. Luckily, I am immune.

"I'll be back in two hours. Hold the fort."

The others were too busy debating case merits to notice my leaving. It's a big condo.

I drove to the casino, navigating light traffic. I valet parked the Jag. I don't have time to mess around. Plus, valet parking leaves a record of me arriving.

I walked slowly and deliberately, making a point of noticing people, especially employees. I was subtle, nobody noticed me back.

Wandering inside, I spotted a nice bar in the corner that wasn't crowded. I used a credit card to buy a drink. More records of my whereabouts.

Casinos permit you to smoke, like I need permission. This is America, right? I remember when everyone let you smoke. It was a more civilized time. I loved the smell of booze, perfume, tobacco, and money permeating the rancid air of a nice casino... it would be nice if the noise wasn't so annoying though. That 'ding-ding-ding' and the constant four to five second blips of music-like noise emitted by all the slot machines, nearly sounding like a song, then not. Every tone of each electronic sound is designed to create a sense of urgency, despair, and anxiety... the slightly brighter than normal flashing lights almost imperceptibly flicker at a coordinated rate, hypnotizing the guests into a sense of detachment and single-mindedness, compelling them to gamble, or gamble faster for those already hooked. It's an evil sound partnered with demonic lights. Luckily, I know that subliminal devil for what it is and ignore it, or at least I try to. I'm not trying to get Biblical here but those sounds and the lights are a big part of what put the 'sin' in the word 'casino.'

Scanning the main room, I searched for the highest ranking security guy, one of the professional types, a boss, not a goon. I spotted him across the lobby eyeballing a couple who might be preparing to pull off a slip-fall scam. I've seen the type before... they're easy to spot. I think they will be wishing they really fell flat on their back on a marble floor if they pull a fake flop in front of this guy.

His eyes swiveled like a hawk, garnering the attention of his 'associates.' He did a quick side-nod of his head in the direction of the con-artists. It's always the tiny gestures that capture attention in a crowd. I don't know why.

Suddenly five big goons appeared from nowhere and bum rushed the couple out the front door, stuffed them in a cab, and might have dispensed a fat lip or two on the way. It happened fast. Professional. Clean... I respect that. Problem averted.

I slipped the bartender a hundred bucks. "What's that guy's name, pal?" I asked.

"Who?"

"Sasquatch over there." I gave a head nod in the security man's direction.

"Gilheaney... Doyle Gilheaney... why?"

"Irish," I commented without inflection.

The bartender smiled, "Very... he likes to drink and fight. I think he found the job he was born to do."

Gilheaney was a significantly larger man than I in bulk and height. I'm carrying some fat, his muscles have muscles. The word 'beast' comes to mind as I looked at him. He looked like a gorilla stuffed into a human suit, with extraordinarily long arms connected to a stocky, barrel-chested body and a huge block head. His face looked like it once was intimate with the front bumper of a fast-moving city bus, not unlike a lot of professional fighters I've known. He appeared to be one of those guys who needs a shave a half an hour after shaving. Gilheaney had medium length reddish brown hair neatly combed and parted. I noticed he had freckles, which caused me to think about Monica's cleavage again, which I had totally forgotten about.

Even though he was gifted with a beast-body, his dark blue Tom Ford suit was well tailored and looked sharp with the dark gray pinstripe shirt and maroon tie. I noticed he wore black leather dress sneakers, nice looking, but not appropriate with a suit. I think those served a more functional purpose than style though. The imprint of a firearm on his belt was barely visible. Only a professional would notice it. I don't care what anyone else might say, this guy was no slouch, even if he might be missing a few of the steps from the pathway of human evolution.

"I need to talk to him," I told the bartender.

The bartender squirmed like his shorts were too tight. Then he looked into my eyes. I let him see my teeth... he suddenly realized the future of his good looks probably depended on my good will.

"He's actually friendly until he's not. You can just go talk to him. I promise you, it's cool," the bartender swore as he stuffed the c-note in his vest pocket.

"Hardly information worth a hundred bucks, pal," I groused.

"Dude, chill...I'm going to signal him. You're cool," he said as he made a quick wave that caught

Gilheaney's attention followed by a thumbs up and nod.

Although the hand signal was subtle, the security saw it. He doesn't miss a thing. Yeah, he's a professional.

Gilheaney nodded back.

I guess I'm good to go.

I took my drink with me, crossing the room carrying it in my off-hand in case I have to draw and shoot this big bastard. I walked over, switched my drink to the left, and offered my right. He shook it. He seemed to not be as clinically insane as he appeared.

"How may I help you, Mister…" he asked, already starting an interrogation that was all dressed up like common civility. He showed me some perfectly white movie star teeth that must have cost a fortune. I can guess what happened to his originals.

"Becker, just Becker."

"Mister Becker."

I didn't let him know the bartender gave me his name, just in case Gilheaney might be inclined to murder him for doing so. That seemed within the realm of possibility. Also, I think he knew exactly who I am and why I am here. I imagine he is the turd who ordered my previous soiree with the three stooges in the storage room.

"I'd like to have a meeting with Mister Conti… about a personal matter."

"I'm sorry, don't know a Mister Conti."

This guy is good.

Gilheaney's voice was as smooth as Michael Bublé and his movements and facial expressions projected class, intellect, and style. The word incongruous comes to mind. There is something about an extremely polite and articulate brute that is difficult to process. Our conversation so far feels like a 'what's wrong with this picture' puzzle. I noticed his Jorge Adeler cufflinks. A lot of hoods don't do french cuffs. Those links had to set him back about eight grand. He has good taste for a hired leg-breaker, and he must be very well compensated for his services. I'm going to guess he is a very competent leg breaker to make that kind of dough... I'm pretty sure he's not a trust fund baby.

I responded coyly. "Oh, I understood that a Mister Conti was the chief executive of the casino."

I learned long ago that during any investigative conversation, you never place them be in a position to directly deny a fact with a flat yes or no, and thus end the chat. Always frame it in a way that their answer might comfortably be responded to with more questions or compels them to elaborate in their answer. Always dispense with confrontational body language and words. If I went with an accusatory 'yes, you have heard of him, he's your boss,' then our talk would become a direct confrontation which I would obviously lose, and lose quickly. Now he is thinking... we are fencing, flicking our metaphorical foils in the air like two dueling sophisticates in some Dumas adventure story. We are not arguing, we are playing by the rules. This technique seldom works with stupid people. But this guy didn't appear to be even a little stupid, which I found sad. I'm going to have to work for this.

He surprised me by unexpectedly shifted gears. "What is this personal matter you are concerned with? If it is casino business, perhaps I can direct you to someone who can help you. Otherwise, it might be time for you to leave, Mister Becker."

Still no admission of Conti being in the casino. In my peripheral vision I noticed large hulking forms making their way through the crowd to our position. Not what I would call a good sign.

"I want to talk about my client getting murdered in your parking lot."

"Client? That sounds professional."

His face didn't give away any interest, surprise, or alarm. He's good.

"Yeah. And I'd like to keep it professional," I said calmly as I did an eyebrow raise towards the fast-encroaching herd of hostile goon beef.

He gave me a long hard stare and decided not to go with the wild west saloon brawl option. "Fine."

He gave a subtle hand sign to the crew of knuckle draggers and they all turned and disappeared into the crowd. I polished off my drink in celebration.

"You are talking about Sonechka?" he asked, looking more concerned than defensive this time.

"Yeah... She was a nice kid, caught in your casino gangster drama... Totally unnecessary."

"*Not* gangsters, Becker. We don't use the G word here."

"Right... then you're what... associates?"

"This isn't what you think it is, Becker. I won't let you see Conti, but I'll tell you what I can. Why don't we sit down where we can have some privacy."

We strolled like old pals, the kind who walk shoulder-to-shoulder without speaking or making eye contact, over to a quiet corner of one of the many casino bars. The people in the surrounding tables got up and left on cue, like they rehearsed it, as we sat down. He noticed my glass was empty. "Drink?"

"Yeah, I need one."

He did a fancy set of quick hand signals that included a point at the bartender, a glass-holding gesture, a victory sign, and a point to a location. within a minute two drinks arrived, delivered by a leggy cocktail waitress with a set of highly visible elite gazoombas, generously taunting us as she leaned over the table to sit down our drinks.

Gilheaney tipped her a hundred bucks. "Thanks, Brittany."

She giggled as she stuffed the Benjamin

somewhere between her knockers. She probably had room to open a savings and loan in there.

I turned my attention back to my host. "I don't think a move happens in this joint unless it's already choreographed, Mr..."

"...Gilheaney. You wouldn't be far wrong to think so, Becker."

I decided to show some cards. He made a step in the right direction, I felt it was appropriate to reciprocate. "I'm a licensed private investigator. I was hired to find a missing girl, a friend of Sonechka..."

"I know her... Monica."

"Makes sense. She worked here."

"Did you find her?"

He slipped up, sounding a bit too anxious to know her location.

"No, not yet," I lied. I'm trying to be courteous, but this guy hasn't really proven to me that I shouldn't shoot him in the eye socket yet.

Gilheaney tried hard to sound unconcerned again. "She was Luca's girl. This is all a huge misunderstanding."

"Luca, the guy who burned up in a car trunk? Yeah, I can see how he misunderstood."

Gilheaney bristled, "Don't be a wise ass, Becker. I'm trying to help you."

"Then help me... what the fuck is going on?"

"First, I know who you are. I heard about you smoking that dirtbag in that Pompano Beach mall a couple of years ago, and then all that Columbian Cartel shit last year. You were a cop once. One of the honest ones. But still a goon."

"I've had my moments."

"And then, you came in here and fucked up three of my guys, not our best and brightest, but still... gutsy move. You earned some respect with my legit security team. They been watching the video on their breaks for laughs."

"Thanks. I figured it might be an audition for some work."

"Maybe... but let's not get ahead of ourselves. Here's the deal. Someone is making moves on us... very heavy handed. The girl knows who it is... we need her alive, at least until we talk to her. I don't even know at this point if she is one of them or not. Is that helpful enough?" He punctuated his question by taking a long sip from his cocktail while staring over the glass with eyes that were deader than an alligator rolling up on a drowning raccoon.

"Yeah, fair enough. So now that we're having a 'professional' conversation, I'll give you this tidbit of news. I did find her... but, don't get excited. She's in the wind again."

"Too bad," he said like a guy who just heard a blatant lie, but could live with it.

I ignored his response to my lie and continued. "She told me it was cartel guys from the Mexican border cartels, not Columbian assholes, the

Mexican frontier guys… but I think she was made it all up."

"Why would she?"

"She's a woman… she's in trouble… and she barely knows me. She'll do anything, including misdirecting me, to save herself. Plus, the MO doesn't add up. A border crew will just shoot you in the face and then take a whiz on your twitching corpse… or maybe leave a head in a burlap sack in front of the casino. They don't do bombs on a first date."

"True. Do you have the magician?"

Gilheaney quickly changed gears, shifting away from the cartel story. I don't know if that means anything. Maybe he's just very direct conversationalist, or maybe he's hiding something.

"I know where he is." I confessed, providing some truth but not the whole truth , full stop.

"Does he know anything?" he asked.

I decided to go with the whole truth on this one. "No… he is shocked as anyone else. They killed his girl in that bomb blast. He's pissed."

His facial expression changed from granite to molasses. He was about to reveal something he felt. Something out of character for this kind of situation. These kinds of guys don't drop their guard… ever.

Gilheaney raised his glass to his lips, then put it down without drinking. "Damn it. I'll be real honest here, Becker. I like that guy... he's a decent man and he's a big hit here with our clientele... an amazing magician. Usually, I hate all that magic shit, but he is something else. I barely knew his girl, but please let him know we will take care of any arrangements and costs. She was part of the company. We're assholes, but we're not total assholes."

That told me that Gilheaney might be more than a top tier security man in this place. Offering to expend funds for a funeral, talking about personnel like an executive management knob would, there was more to him than I thought. But what? He's definitely a role player.

I slipped him a card. "Thanks. I get it. Look, let me do my thing. I'll stay out of your way, you stay out of mine... here's my phone number. Call me if you get something. I'd be happy to call you if I get something."

Gilheaney took the card, looked at it as fondly as you'd look at a written death threat slipped under your door, then with a show of faux reluctance, gave me his card. "Deal, gumshoe. It's a deal until it isn't."

I nodded. "I still want to talk to Conti."

"I'll see what I can do."

"Until then."

He didn't respond. He just looked at me like I overstayed my welcome.

I carefully stood up from my chair while he

remained seated, his gun hand low and out of sight... we weren't really allies yet, just one of those 'the enemy of my enemy' things... I like it that way.

A quick about-face pointed me towards the door and I left. I think this is going to be one of those cases where nothing good happens... not that anything good *ever* happens once a private investigator is called.

CHAPTER 4 - ESCAPE AND EVASION

I'm calling this little visit a win. It feels good to leave a situation like this without a fat lip or stab wound. I lit up a cigarette as I stood outside, making smoke ring tributes to the night sky gods, while waiting for a valet to bring my car around. The night air was damp and salty, exactly the way I like it. Life is good.

As I waited for my car, a skinny chick with green hair and a nose piercing walked towards me accompanied by a flabby guy squeezed into skinny jeans with the cuffs rolled up like a farmer and sporting a man-bun.

Green hair gave me a look a normal person might use if they stepped on a fresh dog turd. "Nobody smokes anymore, boomer," she snarled.

I didn't even bother looking at her, "Fuck you, beatnik." Then I turned and blew a fat smoke cloud in her face.

She gave me the official Greta 'How dare you face,' then looked at her boyfriend, expecting he would defend her honor.

He thought about it... I could see him mentally trying to convert his video game fighting skills into real life, but reality is a harsh master.

The boyfriend might be a pussy, but stupid? No, he is not stupid. He quickly concluded that I might not react well to aggression, and he obviously didn't want to spend his gambling money on reconstructive dental work, so he kept his mouth shut and just squirmed uncomfortably. He might have wet his pants a little.

The doormen responded out of nowhere, briskly 'guiding' the pair into the casino before the she-puke could do whatever beatniks do when their indignant little heads explode. This joint has top-tier professional staff... I'll give that to them.

A valet rolled up in my Jag. He gingerly exited and jogged towards me with my keys in his hand. He was a nice-looking kid, maybe twenty, short hair, clean shaven, his uniform was sharp and pressed. Maybe the cops should recruit him.

"Have a nice evening, sir."

"Thanks, kid."

I tipped the youngster twenty bucks and hopped in behind the wheel. I needed to get to the safe house and write some shit down.

I drove the speed limit. It was nice enough to turn off the air conditioning, roll down the windows, and open the roof. Something about that ocean air at night fires up what's left of my brain cells. I changed my mind about the safe house and took a drive north along the coast.

Traffic was light, which was a nice change.

I got to the far side of Lighthouse point and

turned back and drove south to almost Miami.

There had to be something I'm missing. Is someone lying? Probably. Is everyone lying? Possibly. The only one I trust outside my crew is Nicolo. We worked patrol together. That means something, at least it does to retired cops.

But what about Monica and her freckled cleavage, which just now came into my mind for no reason. Monica Brand might know more than she's saying. She's the little cotter pin holding this calamity of a case together.

I'd like to question her again, but I don't have enough verifiable information to push back against any lies. Maybe Nicolo could help fill in some blanks on her. It was time to go to the safe house and have another chat.

A right, another right, one more right and a left had me northbound again. That's when I spotted the tail.

But who was it? I didn't feel like Gilheaney would put a crew on me. Maybe it was the bad guys... whoever the hell they are.

It wasn't time to play a highway game with them yet. I turned into one of the ubiquitous gas station and market combinations and parked, then waited. The car tailing me went by like nothing happened. But another car pulled in and parked across the lot. It had two guys in it. I'm not an expert but they looked like a couple of assholes. Just kidding... I've dealt with enough assholes to have a proctology license.

I wandered into the market and picked up a cup of coffee. I spotted the first car staged down the street. The double asshole ride was still sitting in the parking lot trying to act disinterested... like a couple of big slobs in suits sit in parking lots late at night in a... well, we are close to Miami Beach... but... I stood there sipping my delicious gas station coffee and stared at them. They needed to know their cover was blown.

I walked back to the trunk of my car and popped it open.

They split, probably expecting me to pull a twelve gauge out and smoke their sorry asses. I was really just getting out a little airplane bottle of Jim Beam to freshen up my coffee. But I was really hoping they thought I might be escalating our little game. It worked.

The other car disappeared too. Was there a third I didn't spot? Why were they following me? I don't want to get tunnel vision. It might be a different case. I've pissed off a lot of people over the years. If they were cops, I probably wouldn't have made them so fast. An undercover police crew would probably run a five to seven car surveillance and use might even use an airplane if it was important enough.

Maybe Monica Brand knew. I had a feeling she might.

I hit the street again doing a few evasive moves,

then parked and called a ride share to drive me a few blocks away. I walked back to near where my car was and watched to see if someone was sitting on it. I looked up for drones or a circling airplane.

Nothing.

I got back in the Jag and headed to the safe house, throwing in a few more runs down cul-de-sacs and alleys to scare up any lingering doubts that I lost them, or they just gave it up.

Ten minutes later I made my way back to the safe house.

I received a warm greeting upon my arrival.

"Where the hell have you been, Becker?" Mother Hen Vance had her hands on her hips like I was getting in late from the prom drunk and pants-less.

"Casino." It's always wise to use one word responses when under interrogation by an angry woman. The more you talk, the worse it gets.

"Are you nuts?"

"Yes."

She gave me her cute snarl that said she was just worried, not angry. "Don't be cute. You need to take a cover team with you next time. You're not bullet proof, Becker. You can die as easily as the rest of us." She gave me an affectionate arm punch which meant that if I play my cards right, the lecture is over.

"So far I haven't died. So, I probably won't in the future either…. do you want to hear what I found out or not?"

She calmed, "Yeah, I do."

We walked to the kitchen and I pulled a couple of breakfast beers out of the refrigerator. Then I came to my senses and grabbed two more and the bottle opener.

We parked our butts in the living room. I loosened my tie and told her everything. The casino, the green-haired hippy, and the tail.

Joan is a professional. She took the whole story in without speaking. After letting the thoughts percolate for a few minutes, she came to a conclusion that was exactly the same as mine. "Something else is going on here, Becker."

"Yeah… something else. And we have no idea what it is yet."

Joan took a long pull on her beer then updated me on the conversation they had during the evening. "Nothing new came of it. I think we need to talk to Nicolo privately."

"Do you think he's hiding something?"

"No, I think he's still in shock over Sonechka. The two of them were inseparable. From what I understand they were a fairly popular couple with the crowd and the staff at the casino too. None of this sounds like a cartel job. At least, not with what we know so far."

"What do you want to do?"

I trust Joan's expertise. You don't go the Los Angeles County Organized Crime Task Force as a supervisor without having some significant investigative chops. But I was afraid she was going to say the words I was thinking. I polished off my first beer and then immediately regretted not bringing three each.

Joan stole a cigarette out of my pack on the coffee table. "Becker, this smells like mob action."

I snorted. "Yeah... I know."

"Which bunch?"

"It has to be Atlantic City, Vegas, or Los Angeles."

"Why?"

"Atlantic City and Vegas would be interested in the Casino angle and Los Angeles is stupid enough to make a move like this."

"L.A. isn't so stupid anymore, Becker. After that asshole Don Carloto guy slipped, hit his head, and died, the old boys came back and took over. They're too smart to try this."

"Slipped and hit his head?"

"Yeah, it was a convenient lie. But that's what the coroner went with."

I chuckled. *You got to love those mob guys.*

"Do you mind asking your friend Mister Stump about it? Would he even say?"

"He'd just say there was no such thing as organized crime and tell me to forget about it."

"I guess we'll need to do this ourselves then."

"Yeah, like always."

We drank beer and talked until the first light of dawn. I heard some stirring in the back. Worm stumbled out looking like a cat puked him up.

"I'll make some breakfast," he announced as he unsteadily made his way to the kitchen. Worm is not a morning person.

"Did you sleep?"

"No, too much going on.. I just tossed and turned."

"Grab a shower before you head to the kitchen. We already started drinking breakfast."

"Good idea..." he staggered back down the hallway and disappeared like a sinking boat into the night.

Joan got up. "I'm going to shower too, Becker. You should get some sleep."

"After Worm comes back and makes breakfast, I'm going to crash for a few hours."

"Sounds like a plan." She turned and started towards the back.

"Hey Vance."

"Yeah."

"Thanks for worrying."

"I wasn't worrying. If you get killed, I don't get paid. That's self-preservation, pal."

I laughed... she winked... I think we had what people call 'a moment.'

I walked out to the main balcony and watched the sky glow as the sun came up over the Atlantic. Florida is the gift that keeps on giving, whatever the hell that is supposed to mean. But it is my home. Between the crazies, the geezers, the conmen, the hustlers, the hacks, and the normal bastards just trying to make their way through life, there is nowhere else like it. Why would anyone ever leave this place?

I sat down in a deck chair and pondered the existence of the universe. A man's hand on my shoulder startled me with a soft shake. It was Worm.

"Wake up, boss. Breakfast is on. You dozed off."

"No I didn't. I was meditating."

"You can't meditate and snore. That's science, Becker."

The aroma of bacon refocused my thoughts, directing me to eat rather than bicker with Mister Worm.

I took a shot at winning our debate. "Science is for pussies."

Worm, the consummate butler retorted. "I agree."

Wisdom...

I got a plate of scrambled eggs and bacon, dumped shredded feta cheese on it and drenched it in salsa. The coffee smelled strong enough to arm wrestle Dick Butkus. I grabbed a cup. The aroma crawled up my nostrils and karate chopped my nose hair... mmmmm...

The others, minus Joan, came out and joined us.

Tiki was dressed and ready for the day. It is difficult to determine if Dourdhoff is dressed for the day or not, he always looks the same. I think he sleeps in his clothes. Nicolo and Monica came out. They didn't have fresh clothes. I'd get them some today. Nicolo was wearing what he had on last night. Monica was wearing a plush bathrobe from the closet. It was not tightly closed. Those freckles... what is the deal with those?

I was having some reaction that guys my age shouldn't have around a woman her age. I decided to remain seated at the table and finish my meal until things cooled down.

Monica gave me a cute mini-grin and leaned over to give me a hug. "Good morning, Becker. Thanks for getting me to safety last night."

Her hug came in from the right side as she acted like nothing out of the ordinary was happening. From the corner of my eye, I couldn't help but see an almost complete breast, or as we in the detective business call them, a boob. I tried not to see it, but there the thing was.

How do women know when they are making mister happy come to attention? Why do they exploit the situation? Why am I so nervous about this?

I tried to play it off. "Just part of the job, Monica. I'm glad you're safe." I scooted my chair in closer to the table to discourage any additional hugs and to conceal my current condition.

She winked at me again, then assembled a breakfast plate and went back to her room.

Women are unpredictable.

I finished my breakfast and a cup of coffee. It was time to get some sleep. It might seem odd to drink coffee and go to sleep in the morning afterwards, but it is not unusual in the detective business to be completely out of synch with the rest of the world. All the beer I drank will counteract the coffee. I'm a professional. I know what I'm doing.

I walked back to the last vacant bedroom and locked the door behind me. I don't know why I locked the door. But it seemed like the thing to do.

Four hours later I was shaved showered and dressed for the day. Worm was waiting for me with more coffee and a tray of sandwiches.

Everyone else had their faces in screens, looking at who knows what. Durd noticed me first.

"Becker. Something interesting about the casino board."

I took a big slug of hot coffee before talking. "Yeah, what?"

"They're losing money. In a casino... they're bleeding margin."

"What?"

Durd spun the screen around and showed me. Yeah, it looked bad. "What's causing it?"

"Only two things that I can think of and I can't prove either one yet. Someone is embezzling in a big way or outsiders were laundering cash through the joint and the tap was turned off... right here."

He pointed to a point on the chart dated four months ago. This kind of suspicious financial activity would have state and federal inspectors charging in next quarter like Patton rolling into Messina."

"Does somebody own a government official?" I asked.

"Could be..."

Durd seemed uncertain. Durd never seems uncertain. This is not a good sign.

I put a fine point on my question. "So, who's the bad guy?"

"Unclear. The villain at this point could come from inside *or* outside. I'll need more time and maybe a forensic auditor to help me."

I thought about for a second before answering. "Have Joan send it to Mister Stump in Los Angeles. He's ten times better at spotting a mob angle than any of these college boys."

"If it's the mob behind this, won't he have a conflict of interest?"

I guess I should have thought about it two or three more seconds. "Good point. And let's not ever mention to him that I used the word mob and him in the same sentence."

"Yeah, that never happened as far as I'm concerned."

I asked, "Who else do we have."

"We could call Rochester Billington?" Durd

suggested in the form of a question.

"Rochester? That stuffed shirt? He's the most obnoxious blowhard aristocrat snobby two-bit jackass in Florida."

"He's good."

He is good... dammit!

"Send it to him then. We need answers."

I personally despise Rochester. He thinks everyone is riff-raff except his little band of trust fund babies he has lunch with at Breaker's every Tuesday... and never invites me, even though we went to high school together... I guess because I once gave him a wedgie in the fourth grade. I'm ready to forgive and forget, but apparently, he holds a grudge. I might even be richer than him now but that aristocrat blue blood attitude supersedes bank account status. I hate snobs. Their patrician attitude is unmerited and unbearable... it's also undefeatable, at least with conventional weapons. If you give them the finger, they just pick up a coffee cup and point their pinky finger at you. If you tell them to 'eff off,' then they just lift their nose and say, "bish-posh, old man," whatever the hell that means... who even says 'bish-posh' except these bastards? Nothing fazes them. Maybe Durd can handle him, and I won't have to deal with that rude jerk.

I put Rochester out of my mind and started thinking about next moves. I wanted to have a private talk with Nicolo. Joan had a lead to run down with Tiki. I wondered if I should knock on Monica's door and check on her but the thought of it made me feel weird and disoriented, so I used good judgement for a change and abandoned that idea.

I addressed my old police department buddy. "Nicolo, let's go out and get a coffee and talk."

He gave me a thumbs up. He was wearing a disguise, a local football team jersey and a ball cap, the most un-magician outfit there is. We were going to a local diner so I didn't expect we would see any mobsters or casino hoods there.

Ten minutes later we were in a back booth sipping coffee and waiting for six orders of bacon with a side of bacon.

"Nicolo, tell me from the beginning. What's the story of you and the girls, you and the casino, the whole thing."

Nicolo sipped at his coffee before talking. "I was retired. I always did magic since I was a kid. I decided to try to make money at it."

"Did you always have a fez?" I had to ask. I saw him wearing it at his show and thought it was cool.

"Yeah, it was either fez or turban... you know how it is."

I didn't, but I acted like I did and just nodded knowingly.

He continued, "I started getting some small jobs, then some corporate jobs... Sonechka and I had been dating and she joined my act. She was beautiful and had some comedy chops... After a couple of years, I auditioned for the casino and scored a gig. The act developed and we blew up big... we were a major feature at the casino. We even got a late-night television spot on the Colesto Show once... we had national act potential. She loved the glamour and attention, but for me, I was always about the magic, Becker. The comedy and sexy stuff with Sonechka was a cool addition to the act, but I am a professional magician."

"Did that cause some friction with you guys?"

"No, more of an internal thing for me. The more successful you are, the less they let you do. The booking agents don't like new stuff, just the stuff that is proven to entertain. It's a little frustrating to me."

"So, you are saying that magic is real?" I said cautiously in case it was. I didn't want to get turned into a frog.

"No... yes... magic is real, it's not supernatural. There are ten elements of magic to master. It's all about misdirection, illusion, and leveraging the willingness of people to believe what they think they see, not what they really see."

"I don't understand a word you said except it's not supernatural... and it's not, right?"

"Right." he grinned. "And if it was, I wouldn't tell you."

"Fucker."

He laughed out loud for the first time since the

car bombing.

It was a much-needed break from his despair, but a brief one.

The waitress arrived with our big plate of bacon. I don't know why diner air is better than any other air but it has to have something to do with the essence of syrup, bacon, and fried egg molecules floating through the air. It makes me not even care that my fork looks like it was still wearing part of the last guy's scrambled egg. Cleanliness might be next to godliness, but diner ambiance is standing on its shoulders looking down with a stack of pancakes.

"Nicolo, I need to know everything. From the beginning. You were together with Sonechka, but didn't know Monica before the casino, right?"

"Right."

"So, let's go back to you and Sonechka getting together."

"Okay. All the way to the beginning. Sonechka and I met at a birthday party at Sea Watch. You've been there, right?"

"A bunch of times. I love that place."

"Yeah, it's the best." He went on with his story, "It was a birthday party for Johnson... remember him? Traffic division. Big motor cop. Black guy."

"Yeah, I remember Johnson," I chuckled. "I once saw him rip a guy through the driver's window with one hand for spitting on the ticket after he signed it."

"Yeah, he was a bad ass. I remember that incident too. After Johnson pulled him out of the car he wasn't sure what the charge was for spitting on a ticket, so he shoved him back in the window, then let him leave with his copy of the spit coupon and a load in his shorts."

"Johnson was a true problem solver. A great guy."

"He lives in Mobile, now."

We both took a sip of coffee in honor of the good old days. But I had to get the conversation back on topic.

"What happened next with you and Sonechka?"

"We hit it off so, I asked her out. One thing led to another. I had a gig at the Moose Lodge, and she went with me... I think she was a big hit with those guys. Bigger than my act... so, from then on, she was part of the show... then we started having some success... very quickly."

"Wow... I never knew much about your second career. I thought it was a hobby."

"It sort of was, then someone in the entertainment industry spotted us at a show and it took off. We've been a regional hit in the southeast for a while, but we could pop nationally at any time."

"Cool. How did Monica fit in?"

"When we scored the Casino gig, we met her. Sonechka and Monica became friends.... very close friends."

I noticed he said that in an odd way, like he was embarrassed or had something to hide. "How close, Nicolo?" I lit a Lucky Strike to put a little smoke between us. I found that having the smoke cloud between two people talking will provide a mental veil, a filter to protect the speaker from the rough spots in a conversation.

Nicolo stared into his coffee, leveraging a fat pause before speaking. "Uh, look Becker... This can't go beyond you and me."

"We worked patrol together, brother."

He took a deep breath and nodded.

That was enough to satisfy him of my loyalty.

"Her and Sonechka... Monica and Sonechka... they had a bit of a romantic relationship on the side. Once in a while... you know how it is in show business."

I don't know how it is in show business. I don't want to know.

"On the side?" I asked.

"And with me... once in a while."

"Oh." I said a little more sharply than I meant to. That was a shocking revelation and I think I failed to conceal my surprise at hearing it.

I had a newfound respect for Nicolo. He didn't seem the type to have two women at once... a lot of traffic cops can only have a personal relationship with their motorcycle and can only experience intimacy as biologically necessary with women in order to create more motor officers. At least that was my opinion. I was a goon squad guy... I never really related to motor officers. But I was always glad to see them when the shit hit the fan. They all seem to enjoy fighting.

Wait... Am I experiencing envy? Of course not... but I'm old, not dead. My imagination is frolicking in the land of erotic thoughts about the two girls thing, but the image of a naked Nicolo involved kept slamming it into oblivion.

I quit letting my mind wander and refocused. Something was happening here. Nicolo was sheepish about this admission. I sensed he wasn't entirely comfortable with his romantic situation.

"Was that working out okay, man? I mean, this is the era of the second sexual revolution. Not judging." In reality, I was judging but I couldn't let him know that.

"To tell you the truth, Becker, it was a little weird... amazing and cool, but weird and uncomfortable. I'm a simple guy... I was raised Presbyterian, not Episcopalian."

I had no idea what that religious reference met... and I wasn't sure he did either. "So, was there trouble?"

"Not really... like you would think there could be. We kept it confidential. Monica started helping with the act, which made us even more popular with the customers... and the boss..."

His voice drifted off and he stared over my shoulder at the door. A guy with a background in psychology might think he was subconsciously fantasizing about escaping this conversation. But I'm an old retired cop. I think he wants to tell the next part, but he knows saying it will change some things. I've seen it before, when a suspect is about to confess to a crime, they get that look and stare at the door. The look doesn't mean escape. It means that a door is about to open and something bad is coming through it.

"What happened, Nicolo?"

"Luca... Luca had an interest in her. He started insisting we make her a bigger part of the act. He started asking her out. Then she only showed up when it was time for a show. Sometimes she didn't appear for the show... then she rarely appeared. We didn't see much of her after that. I think it bothered Sonechka. She felt betrayed... maybe not betrayed... abandoned by her friend."

"And you?"

"I missed her too... but in spite of what was going on behind closed doors, I only cared about Sonechka romantically. I loved her. Monica was just an added... value? Is that the right word?"

"How the hell should I know what the right word is?"

He snickered. "Yeah, I know... any other guy would be in heaven in that situation... and it was nice... but the only woman for me was Sonechka. I wanted to get married. She wanted to wait for a while... especially after her relationship with

Monica changed... it bothered her."

This kind of stuff is why nobody likes women. Even women don't like women. Yeah, I haven't had a girlfriend in a while.

A waitress came by and freshened our coffees. It was an excuse for both of us to shut up and think for a bit.

I took a restroom break and came back. My buddy was just staring in his coffee like a guy with a hole in his shoe. "Nicolo... who else knows all this?"

"Monica...otherwise, no one that I know of."

"Sonechka never told anyone?"

"No, she was a very private person, really, in spite of being amazing on stage... she never spoke of it to anyone other than me."

"Did you have a problem with Luca?"

"I barely knew the guy. He liked to act like he was some kind of gangster, always trying to intimidate everyone, but he left me alone... the only thing we ever discussed was business."

"Was he an asshole?"

"He was definitely an asshole. Maybe even a total asshole. I couldn't understand what Monica saw in him...unless it was money."

"So where are things with you and Monica now... how does that... relationship... stand since Luca came on the scene?

"Between us, Becker?'

"Yeah."

"She stuck around about once a month after we did the show and the three of us would have a night together. Usually when Luca was out of town. But she was always more interested in Sonechka rather than me. I could have been easily replaced with any guy, I think, as far as Monica was concerned. Monica is a sexual animal. She's got this erotic thing about her. She makes things steamy... or she can be ice cold. But for right now, we are still co-workers, friends... somewhat... no animosity... but no passion either, at least that I sense."

"Look, I'm not criticizing or judging, but earlier she seemed to be a little clingy with you... I'm not sure how to explain it."

"Yeah, that's what I mean by steamy. She can take something innocent, like comforting a friend, and make it look like porn music should start playing. She has something... I don't know the word... seductive about her..."

"Besides the long red hair and big boobs?"

I'm a detective. I had to ask.

"Yeah. Something... like an animal. Everything she does is sexy."

"Interesting..."

"Yeah, Becker... it's interesting... but what has that got to do with the car bomb?"

"Maybe nothing. But I got to know what we're dealing with."

"No one else gets these details though, right?"

"Of course not."

I might have just lied. Vance will need to know. But not just yet.

I started edging out of the booth. "Let's get back to the others. It's time to get back to work."

"Yeah. I need to take a dump." Nicolo announced.

The smooth charm of a traffic cop never fails to impress.

"I'll get the car and meet you out front."

I tossed a hundred bucks on the table to cover the tab and to help out a hospitality worker. The story I just heard was worth the c-note.

As we pulled up to the safe house, I got an inbound call, no caller ID. I gave Nicolo a glance, he shrugged. I took the call.

A raspy voice said three words, "Becker, it's Gilheaney."

"Yeah."

"Conti will see you."

"On my way."

I stuffed the phone back in my pocket. "Nicolo, I got to go talk to a guy. Why don't you wait here at the condo."

"Yeah, good idea. I got to go see about destroying a toilet."

"Again?"

"Yeah... Some jobs require follow-up work."

"Uh... I'm not sure that kind of news flash

requires an announcement."

Nicolo flashed me a nasty grin... the kind a motor cop gets when the license check on a traffic stop comes back suspended. He muttered something that sounded like, "Sorry, not sorry," then hopped out of the Jag.

I turned the car around and headed back to the casino. I guess I have to admit that I still have it. I'm probably the best detective in Florida... if not the world. I just worked my way through their turd-level security, their professional top-tier security, and now I finally breached the kingpin-level security at the casino, all in what was probably record setting time. I wondered what Conti would have to say. Then I decided I better think up what *I* was going to say... I lit up a Lucky and gave it some serious thought as I drove.

CHAPTER 5 - I WAS IONIZED, BUT I'M BETTER NOW

As I came within about two blocks from the casino, I caught another inbound call… Vance.

"Hey Becker, you playing lone cowboy tonight or do we get to play?"

She sounded a bit put out with me.

"I need you to watch Nicolo and Monica for now. Have Durd stay on research… but you can send Tiki over to cover me, low profile."

"I should be doing that, Becker," she scolded.

I think she worries too much. It's not like I'm a defenseless geezer.

"We need our best and brightest on protection detail until I finish here. Then we'll regroup and close this thing out."

"Still, I'd feel better if I was with you…"

She almost said my first name. That's forbidden. I cut her next words off.

"It's fine, Vance. They want to talk. I am definitely *not* starting any shit with Conti."

"Fine… I'll send Tiki."

Vance disconnected in a bit of a huff. She's so weird about being protective of me. It's almost uncomfortable. But she's the best investigator I ever worked with. She's relentless. I like that. And she's easy on the eyes, so that is a plus around the office, although I rarely look at her.

I valet parked again. After the explosion the main entrance was temporarily moved to the conference center side of the building. The front was still wound up in yellow crime scene tape and full of bomb techs looking for pieces of whatever it is they look for after a bomb goes off. I strolled through the sliding doors like I was walking into grandma's house on Christmas Day. It seemed like it took me three whole steps inside before I picked up an escort of muscle-heads in suits. Four of them boxed me in and took me to an elevator that was concealed behind a structural pillar and a cigarette kiosk.

We all squeezed in. If sardines could talk, they'd explain how this ride felt. It was me and four guys who might have been injected with buffalo hormones in a metal box that stank of Brut and steroids. I'm not sure if steroids actually have a smell, but I don't want to think any further about what else that essence might be.

There was only one button by the door in the metal box and pushing it shot us straight to the penthouse. It's nice being a guest in the penthouse, except for the part about being so close to the roof where doing an involuntary swan dive off the side might come into play.

I stepped out of the lift and onto plush carpet where I surveyed a wide open area full of nothing but open space and windows to the world.

They must have had massive air filters in this level. Everything smelled ionized. The casino seemed clean until I came in here and saw the true meaning of clean. I wondered if they had a Marine Corps Recruit Depot Sergeant in charge of the janitors in this level.

The lighting here was better too. A lot better. I could see more sharply than normal. Weird stuff going on.

We marched in loose formation to a sterile post-modern office in the back half of the vast entry hall. I slowed as we approached twin doors that surprised me when they opened automatically. Through the door I saw a massive room with a a desk so big that a dozen Cubans could slap an outboard on it and pilot it to Miami. It seems my slowing was unacceptable. A goon accelerated my momentum with a friendly shove in the middle of the back. I briskly entered the office, almost falling on my face in the process.

I re-centered my balance and straightened my tie. My host addressed me with a gracious greeting.

"Mister Becker. I'd say it's a pleasure to meet you... except it isn't."

"I'll concede, I'm not really a popular guy, Conti... Got anything to drink?"

He gangster-chuckled, which is creepy and menacing, then pointed to a pair of hot chicks I hadn't noticed before who were sitting in the corner to my right. One brought me a chair and another brought me a Jack neat in an expensive crystal cocktail glass bearing the casino logo.

I forced myself to ignore the girls and took a seat.

Conti began, "Mister Becker, why don't you tell me where Monica and Nicolo are and we can get on with our lives."

I snapped back, deliberate in my words, but quick to reply. "Why don't you kiss my Irish ass, hood."

Why did I blurt that out? My words were pointlessly dark, unprovoked, and rude. But, that is my style. Maybe my style will finally get me killed tonight.

Surprisingly, Conti laughed. "The 1940s called, they'd like their macho bullshit style back."

I have no idea what that is supposed to mean. I grinned so he would think I did.

"I want them safe, Conti. I'm not working an angle. Nicolo is a friend." *I hate telling the truth to hoods. I'm not sure Conti is really a hood, but he is certainly has a lot of hood charisma.*

"We're on the same page, Becker," he said as he lit up a cigarette and leaned back in his black leather throne, I mean desk chair.

I wasn't so sure we were in the same book, let alone the same page. "So, why play tough, Conti. Let me in on why this is happening." His next words surprised me. I don't get surprised often.

"I agree." He reached in a drawer and removed a

bundle of what appeared to be hundred-dollar bills wrapped in a rubber band. He tossed the wad of cash to me. "Fifty thousand. It's a retainer. I'm a client now, Becker."

I caught the flying cabbage and felt the heft of the money. It was twenties and felt like about five or six pounds, so the count was good. For a moment I thought about throwing it back at him like a righteous hero. But fifty-grand is fifty-grand, even if you are already rich... and besides, Conti was growing on me. I placed the wad on the floor beside me and took a sip of my cocktail before asking my next question, which was pertinent. "Client for what?"

"Someone is making moves on us, Becker. We think it might be West Coast guys with some new partners. They whacked Luca..."

He tossed me a file.

I opened it.

The file contents were significantly superior to what we used to get at the police department intelligence unit. Photos, very clear photos... biographies, vehicles... everything but motive.

"What's this about... what do you mean when you say, making moves... and why?"

"They're making a cash grab before the government puts an end to money. They seem to believe they can launder digital funds and cash simultaneously through our system. Possibly in a way no government agency can trace."

"Can they, if they had access to your technology?"

Conti paused, and then posed a question of his own before answering mine. "I'm a client and what I tell you is confidential, right?"

"You *are* a client," I stated flatly.

He gave me a long cold stare into the eyes that could have knocked a raccoon on meth off a garbage can. Then he sniffed once and his face went slack.

"Then, yeah. We can do that," he admitted... which was scary since it constituted about fifty potential federal crimes if they executed against their capabilities... but being 'able to' and 'doing' are two different things.

I took another sip of my drink to wash down that thought, then asked. "Why don't they just buy you out? They should probably be able to do that. Real gangsters aren't supposed to do gangster shit anymore."

"They tried to buy us. We refused. We know what we got here. What we can do with hard cash and crypto is extremely valuable. We're talking ten digit valuable."

I decided since things are going so swimmingly, I might as well toss a turd in the caviar. "I heard you might have some cash flow concerns."

Conti's face blanched. "Where did you hear that?" He hopped out of his chair faster than if he sat in spilled soup.

"I also hear someone on the inside might be setting your casino up for a hostile takeover."

"Look, Becker... you're way out of line."

"Am I though?"

We had a nice little stare down. I was staring at a guy who knew he was screwed. He was looking at a guy who was not taking 'killing everyone in the room and going home' off the table.

Conti sighed hard... he sat down. "Yeah, there might be a rat."

"Rat is a word a mobster would use."

That earned me a dirty look.

"Listen Becker, we might not all be perfect citizens with sterling character, but we're trying to run this business legitimately. We have a bad apple. I don't know who, and I don't even know what level."

"Can you get me a folder like this on the top three tiers of management?"

"I am a client, right?"

"We already settled that... yeah."

"Done." He pointed at one of the hotties sitting behind us who scrambled out to presumably get what I asked for.

"I need to write something down."

Conti scooted a notepad across his desk.

I scratched out Durd's covert email and scooted it back. "Send it in digital files to this guy. He's part of my agency."

"Not a problem."

It was time to cool our little chat down and refocus on the files he already gave me on dirtbag incorporated.

I thumbed through the photos from the packet. "So who are these clowns?" The faces looked like a stack of portraits from a 1998 Gangster Academy graduation along with some stunt extras out of a Hong Kong karate movie. An eclectic mix of turds, dirtbags, and scum weasels.

Conti, now relaxed again, answered. "They are what's left of the Los Angeles nouveau mob that was wiped out a few years back when the old time New York guys took back over. Those old guys aren't part of this scam. This pack of shit-birds partnered with some cartel guys and some crazy Chinese mob guy… general assholes."

"Chinese? Tong or commies?"

"Both." He grinned like he just said something funny.

Maybe it was funny… yeah, that was kind of funny.

Now I gangster chuckled.

I posed my next query. "Where do they operate out of?"

"The mob guys are from Oceanside, California of all places… low profile, building up power and influence."

"Yeah, I been there, years ago. Close to the border, close to Los Angeles… not a bad shot to Las Vegas, Tucson, or Phoenix… it makes sense."

"It would make sense if they weren't so short on brains and so long on muscle, motivation, and arrogance."

"Bad combination."

"Yeah... very bad. What about the Chinese guys?"

"They're based in Miami. We're unclear on their angle, who they are, and how many of them we have to deal with."

"So, don't you really need shooters and bodyguards? I'm a private investigator. I don't do enforcer work."

"Yeah, right. I know all about you, Becker. You were a goon cop. Back in the day they sent your squad to round up the worst habitual criminals, to hunt the worst fugitives, and to keep the street gangs and outlaw bikers in line."

"That's what they say? I thought we were the forefathers of community policing."

He ignored my sarcasm and continued with my biography as he knew it. "So, you are not an enforcer? And what about when you killed that asshole in Boca Raton or wherever a couple of years ago? Oh.. and we know what you did to those Columbians too last year. You might be a private eye, but you're also a private concussion, contusion, and fractured limb factory. You've single-handedly influenced the price of body bags."

I didn't deny it. I took a sip of my drink and

simply said, "I'm flattered."

That got another hood-snicker out of him. He has a good sense of humor apparently. Yeah, I kind of like this maggot. And yes, I am susceptible to flattery.

I continued with a little clarification. "That was for the department, though. I'm not a paid assassin, Conti."

"Call me Gino."

Wow, I'm practically family now.

"I'm not an assassin, Gino," I reiterated.

He looked a little hurt. "Hey, I'm not asking you to assassinate anybody. They aren't presidents or senators... they're assholes. You can just kill these guys. Nobody will even care. Forgetaboutit."

That's one of the few words of Italian I understand. "Look, I'll get them arrested and shipped out of Florida, but I am not a murderer... as compelling as that line of work might be. Let me take my crew and work them. If you want bodies, call your own guys."

"I don't have guys. We aren't mobsters. I have an MBA from Pepperdine. It's just good for business if everyone just *thinks* we're mobsters."

Sounds like something a mobster would say.

"What about Gilheaney?" I asked.

Conti's face took on an almost sheepish visage. "Well, *he* might be a mobster... but he's the only one."

"Are you sure?"

The sheepish grin was joined by the eye roll of guilt.

"Well... there *might* be a few more. But the executive team and board, we're all mostly legitimate businesspeople. We aren't used to our peers getting whacked... and we certainly don't want to get whacked."

"Fair enough. I'll make sure Nicolo and Monica are safe. Then I'll take a look at this crew and get them popped by the police. That will keep you safe. Where are these assholes?"

The question 'where are these assholes' has launched more of my investigations than I care to admit. Especially when I was still a cop.

Conti wrote something on a notepad as he spoke. "We think Miami, holed up right now in a condo they leased through a shell company. There are about ten of them. Three California mobsters and seven Chinese gun thugs. The car bombing brought too much heat... they're laying low."

He subtlety handed me a note with an address, acting as if he suspected someone was watching us who wouldn't approve. I wondered why it wasn't part of the main file he gave me. Maybe it was fresh news. Sometimes I get paranoid.

I accepted the note, shoved it in my pocket without looking at it, and stood up. "I'll be in touch."

We did a brief mumble-handshake combo and I headed for the elevator, unescorted and alone, which was nice.

I don't know why but, on the way down I started to think about bacon... delicious bacon and eggs. The smell, the taste... with coffee...

A ding and a jolt rattled me out of my daydreaming. I probably need a nap. At my age that solves most problems.

I crossed the casino floor. Tiki was at a slot machine, blending in, but watchful of anything happening in the room. She picked up my trail and casually followed me at a short distance, fake-fidgeting with something in her clutch bag. My tiny colleague blended in so perfectly she was almost invisible.

We traversed the longer route through the conference center to the temporary exit.

Outside, I held out my ticket. The valet snatched it from my hand with a little nod and disappeared. I waited patiently in the sun for my car, wondering why I always expect it to be dark when I exit a casino. Tiki stood just outside the doors, dabbing fresh lipstick on her mouth and anxiously glancing at her watch as if she was waiting for someone. She seemed like a casino fixture. For a hot chick, she is skilled at blending into the background, which is more difficult than it might seem.

Then a van rolled up. It wasn't a delivery van or a tourist van... it was a snatch-and-grab-special, like we used at the police department to snag fugitives off the street. A normal person might not recognize it for what it was, but guys like me, who spent years in the legal kidnapping business, knew it without conscious thought. I'd put the bag on a lot of felons over the years using this method.

But today I was the target.

The side door slid open as the van slid to a stop in front of me. Two big slobs with guns and a canvas bag bailed out of the van door. They were dressed in hoodies and jeans with bandanas covering the lower part of their faces. My detective intuition told me these two slobs didn't have my best interests at heart. At least one more was behind the wheel of the van.

I'd been down this road before. Rule one, never let them get you in the vehicle.

They saw an easy target, a large but elderly man. I might be getting a little long in the tooth, I'll give them that. But they missed the 'mean old bastard with aggression issues' part.

I lowered my center of gravity, stepped back, then delivered a devastating front snap kick to the first guy's nuts. The move was something I remembered from my Shotokan karate days. The impact made a noise that hurt to hear. Imagine the sound of a truck tire rolling over a watermelon. Bad guy one imagined it, except it wasn't imaginary. He just froze, holding his crotch, trying to uncross his eyes, and then fell forward in a heap on the concrete. He is probably wondering if the

Vienna Boys Choir had an opening for a soprano.

I rotated my hips, turning to address bad guy two, who already had a meaty paw on my shoulder. He never saw the side kick stomp that bent the side of his knee into an unnatural angle, fracturing bone and ripping tendons along the way.

That wasn't me doing the kicking, it was Tiki. She's quick.

He didn't suffer much though, she spun and delivered a flying backhand to the head, a knee to the kidneys, and followed up with a solid full power elbow to the nose. He folded and went down, rolling over on his back only to catch a finishing punch to the face as my diminutive employee stood over him and nailed him between the eyes with a brutal right and an overly dramatic bloodcurdling kiai, a karate shout, that I think she picked up from Enter the Iguana, or whatever that movie was called. It sounded like an angry tiger growl. But permit me to be quite candid... it was very cool.

"Cool!" I stage whispered, unintentionally giving voice to my thoughts.

"I know," Tiki snarled as she gave me a look at her war face as she stood in a deep stance over her vanquished meatball.

She snapped back into a taller defensive stance and scanned the area for more targets. I already had my Sig Sauer 45 out of my belt holster and in my mitt, but I didn't have a clear target.

I heard movement to my right.

The driver came out of the van with an AA12 automatic shotgun, spouting those immortal words of yesteryear, "Freeze, assholes!"

I could have charged him, shot it out with him, or even tried to negotiate but I decided to go with his suggestion and freeze. He didn't get out of the van pulling the trigger. He wasn't looking for a bloodbath at a casino...he was only there to snatch one or both of us, which didn't work out. So, I think it's safe to assume he is now operating in janitorial mode, cleaning up the mess.

With one hand, he helped nut-crushed guy into the van while Tiki's guy crawled, limped, hopped, and stumbled along with them. They got in, slammed the side door shut, and hauled ass the hell out of there, disappearing into traffic... gone. I think shotgun boy was the most competent member in his crew. He knew how to execute an evacuation. I saw enough of his face to make him as one of the turds in the photo packets Conti gave me.

An awe-struck part-time valet, who I believe was a full-time beach bum, dramatically commented on the battle. "Bitchin!"

Dozens of casino customers were screaming, running, and trying to get invisible. I guess these kinds of things make the average person nervous.

Another valet, a skinny kid with green hair who missed the whole show, rolled up in my Jag.

I yanked him out of the car and then stuffed a hundred-dollar bill in his shirt pocket. "Hey, I know it ain't your fault, but the parking situation here sucks."

He gave me a big-eyed look like a ruptured chicken, if ruptured chickens had green hair. Some people just go through life clueless. It must be nice.

I barked an order to Tiki. "Get in, we'll get your car later."

Tiki popped into the passenger seat, her Beretta Bobcat in hand, and we got the hell out of there too.

My phone was ringing before we hit the street. It was Gilheaney. "What the hell just happened at my casino, Becker?"

He must have been watching this in the monitoring room to be on it that fast. "Bad guys, Gilheaney... Bad guys happened."

"No shit."

"Yeah, snatch and grab team... not the best ones I ever met, but they were very well equipped and had inside intelligence."

"Fuck."

"Yeah."

"Do you want me to send you some guys?"

"We're good. I'll get back to you." I disconnected.

Something about this ambush was wrong... I couldn't put my finger on it.

Tiki's blood was still pumping. "That was one big shotgun, Becker," she said with her thick accent that only appears when she is mad or excited… which is most of the time.

"Yeah… AA12… effective street sweeper, for sure."

"These guys are serious."

"You might want to up your game from that little .22, Tiki."

For some reason, that advice pissed her off. Her diction went from poor to piss poor as it took a flying swan dive into the toilet. I could barely understand her as she ranted at me.

"Where I hide hand cannon in mini-skirt, genius? I not fat like you. I only weigh 95 pounds… What wrong with you, Becker? Why you being ess-ho?"

I attempted contrition. "Sorry, you can carry whatever you want."

She paused for a moment, just long enough to blast me with the female glare of doom. Then she blurted out a demand. "I want AA12… I'll keep it in my car."

"Those things weigh over ten pounds, Tiki."

"Don't care… I'm feisty…"

I know when to hold 'em and I also know when to fold them. "Tell Dourdhoff to get you one… Bill it to the company."

Tiki might have been a victim when I met her years ago, but now she's probably the most alpha person I know. I'm glad she's on my side. Then I thought about that for a moment.

"You *are* on my side, right Tiki?"

She stared straight ahead as she answered with all the passionless disinterest of a pharmacist reciting the side effects of a new prescription. "Always on your side, Becker. You not as big an asshole as everyone says. Just basic asshole."

"Thanks, Tiki... wait... who says that?"

"Everybody... forgetaboutit."

I didn't know she spoke Italian too. I took her advice and forgot about it. I'm not really offended. Being an asshole is my superpower. I just use it for good instead of evil... most of the time.

I pushed some red lights and did a few dead-end heat runs to make sure we weren't followed and made our way back to the condo. Tiki remained silent, staring blankly out the side window like a wife obsessing about her husband failing to take out the trash in a timely manner.

Ten silent minutes later and we were back in the living room, turned conference room, of the safe house condo. Vance was out picking up food and making a 'fresh clothes and necessities' run for everyone. I was glad she was out. I didn't want another lecture about me doing something without her watching over me like the doting owner of a new kitten.

Dourdhoff was busily banging away on a computer keyboard. Nicolo was on the back balcony having a cigarette and cocktail processing grief. Monica was in her room. Mister Worm brought Tiki and I drinks and set out a tray of sandwiches. All was good at the safe house.

"Durd, did we miss anything?" I asked.

He answered without looking up. "Not much. Rochester had his personal assistant call from the street outside the Everglades Club. The message was, he's busy but he will have something for you tomorrow and he wanted you to come up some time for lunch."

"Lunch?"

"Yeah, at the club."

I grunted a noncommittal sound. *The Everglades Club? I forgot about that place. Of course Rochester would be a member... it makes perfect sense. I wonder if a retired cop had ever entered the joint as a guest before.*

Dourdhoff posed an unenthusiastic, unoriginal, but polite question of his own. "Anything new with you?"

I answered with my own absence of enthusiasm. "No... we might have a lead on the bad guy location. That's about it."

Tiki eye-rolled and then blasted me with another opinion I don't recall asking for.

"You mental, Becker. We almost got killed. That is new!"

What the hell is she upset about?

"Killed?" Dourdhoff asked with all the passion of a man discussing humidity in Florida.

Tiki continued making a big deal out of our little scrape with those rude guys in the van. "Yes, killed. Crew tried to kidnap us. Big fight... almost killed."

That seems like a total exaggeration.

Worm, the former criminal, asked a relevant criminal question. "Did the cops show up?"

I answered. "No cops... just a little dust-up in front of the casino."

Tiki didn't let it go. "Big fight... with bag men. Kidnapping!" she elaborated unnecessarily.

I tried to slow this shit show discussion down. "Yes, there was an attempt to snatch us. We rolled them back. They're gone. But I *did* talk to Conti and he gave me a new location we can work."

What's wrong with these people? Obviously, in this line of work you will be on the receiving end of an occasional kidnap or murder attempt, but that is simply part of doing business. I'm not sure why everyone is making a big deal out of it. The main thing is, Conti gave us a lead.

"Who tried to grab you?" Nicolo asked as he wandered in from the balcony to check out the commotion.

I gave him the answer to what he was really asking me. "Three assholes. Not the best crew. Not the worst. They didn't seem like 'car bomber' material though."

Nicolo frowned at my answer. "But they might know something?"

"Yeah... maybe... I don't know. But it's worth

talking to them."

I tossed the files I got from Conti onto the table in front of Durd. "I think the guy in photo number seven was one of the snatch and grab crew."

"I'll go through all this and upload it into the database. I'll get them all identified. Can you ask Conti to send me the video of the kidnap attempt?"

"Yeah, good idea." I texted Conti. He must have had his phone in his hand as he texted right back. I told Durd,"It's on its way. Should have it in half an hour."

"Copy that," Durd said without looking up.

"Good... and if you can, the big puzzle is who is the inside scumbag skimming money and selling out the casino. When we know that name, we can connect the outside hoods with the hit on Luca."

Tiki added, "And our attempted kidnapping."

I gave her my exasperated look, which is the same as all of my other looks. "Our kidnap? They were after me. They didn't even know you were there."

She grinned like a demon gnawing on a sin sandwich, "They know now though."

I had to laugh, "Yeah, I guess they do."

Dourdhoff interjected, "Any idea who they are or which group any of these guys are affiliated with?"

"No, at this point they are random knobs. But the bad news is, they knew us, knew we were there, and probably know we have Monica and Nicolo. So that means inside information."

"From who?" Tiki asked.

"That's the big question. It had to be from someone working in the casino. I'll get Conti to look over his staffing schedule. Maybe he can spot something... someone who took an unexpected day off or someone who came in early. He'd spot an anomaly...That's our best bet right now."

"Are they at that address Conti gave you?" Nicolo asked.

"Maybe... We need to figure that out. If they are at that Miami address, Conti might already have a crew heading there. I told him not to, but he's not one to take suggestions... yet."

"So... what next?"

I wasn't ready to share my developing concern about the case. Concerns or maybe doubt... or both. I decided to just stay the course. "We pay them a visit."

Nicolo stood up. "If they are trying to find me, they know what I look like. Give me a minute and I'll go with you."

"Are you sure? This could get ugly."

Nicolo's jaw tightened. "It's already ugly, Becker."

My ex-cop turned magician pal disappeared into his room. Moments later, some random stranger came out wearing Nicolo's pants. The physical change was slight but the visual change was significant. It was definitely Nicolo, but was it? I wouldn't have recognized him on the street.

"What the hell?" Worm muttered.... "Nicolo?"

He shared a slight grin. "Yeah... slight misdirection and transformation... sometimes during my act I do a transposition with myself, one moment being on stage and the next appearing as an audience member in the crowd, transposition and transformation."

Even his voice sounded different.

Tiki was shocked, "You look so different."

"Just a dental device, fake hair, glasses, and a change of posture, stance, expression, and walk. and of course a different shirt," he explained.

"Cool," Worm marveled.

Nicolo seemed to take pleasure in elaborating. "Simply a basic talent required of spies and magicians. You'd be surprised at the cross-over skills related to investigative work."

Dourdhoff was fascinated, "Like what?"

Nicolo elaborated, "To execute the ten categories of magic tricks, we use misdirection, false interpretation, prestidigitation, presentation of false but reasonably believable conclusions, observation, confusion, vagueness, language management, voice control, misrepresentation, disguise, and faux agreement, or what we call directed concurrence... a spy might add the dark arts of false sincerity, false compassion, false fear, and false interest."

"So like actors?"

"Somewhat, except spies have to write their

own scripts on the fly under adversarial conditions and wield their talents in dynamic situations."

"But you look so different..." Tiki repeated, still in awe of his change of appearance.

"The illusion is simply the confusion one experiences when they look for something and can't see it, although it is right in front of them. The person doesn't expect to see it so they don't... or the reverse of walking through the Everglades and seeing every stick as a snake, because your survival instincts tell you to expect to see a snake. Or not seeing your lost keys while they are right in front of you on the kitchen counter because you are positive there are somewhere else. I'm just managing perception. In a way, it's simply a matter of reading people and being, or not being, what they expect to see. The average observer uses a person's clothes. facial expressions, and speech and create what they believe to be a pretty thorough evaluation of someone. It's how recognition works most of the time on an instinctive level. A magician, and perhaps spies, will deeply analyze things such as clothes, speech, posture, eyes, hair, feet, stance, diction, terminology, cleanliness, alertness, intellect, jewelry, skin, concern, apathy, awareness, car, job, spouse/significant other, perversions, openness in addressing crime or perversion, attitude, fear, sorrow, joy, and ruthlessness and use this techniques to replace or obfuscate reality. Change up a few of those things and one becomes a different person."

I was thoroughly impressed. "Wow!"

Yeah, I said wow. There is more to this magic bullshit than I thought.

Nicolo continued. "Sherlock Holmes, for example, could notice not only that a man was wearing gray slacks, but he noticed the cut and style, the wrinkles, any debris on the pants, stains, the wear patterns, the cleanliness, and even the odor. Others are amazed at his deductions, It's all there to see. If you can't readily explain it, then it is quite easily interpreted as magic. For a disguise, you just leverage that ability in reverse. Does that make sense?"

"Not one bit... but I kind of get it," Dourdhoff said. "So, you are saying it is similar to hypo-familiarity syndrome?"

Only a nerd like Dourdhoff would ask that.

Nicolo smiled. "Very similar... at least the same ballpark."

I hate big words.

Dourdhoff considered Nicolo's response for a moment before saying, "Now I have to worry about a Fregoli delusion."

That made Nicolo chuckle and shrug again. "Perhaps, Durd... Feeling paranoid?"

For some reason that made Durd chuckle.

This kind of crazy talk is exactly why nobody likes smart people.

Nicolo wrapped up his lecture with, "Yeah, being a magician is more complex than you'd think. At least being a 'good' magician. I just don't just pull rabbits out of hats." Then he lifted Worm's captain hat off his head and pulled a small stuffed bunny toy out of it."

The unusual happened next. A crew of hard-nosed professional detectives started clapping like trained seals begging for a mackerel, grinning and giggling like schoolgirls.

Nicolo bowed slightly and smiled. "Of course showmanship is important too."

"You're amazing, brother. No wonder you are killing it at the casino." I no sooner said it than I realized it was a poor choice of words. But Nico has a cop's sense of dark humor so instead of getting pouty, he just half-laughed and shrugged.

"So, what's our next step, Becker?" Worm asked.

Everyone seemed more enthusiastic and upbeat all of the sudden. Maybe I should schedule regular magic shows.

I answered Worm's question. "We do some light surveillance on this new address and try to catch a break."

Monica appeared in the hallway leaning against the wall. I don't know how long she had been standing there.

"I'm going," she announced. She casually took a sip of her coffee and then took a seat at the table, literally and metaphorically.

"Not a good idea, Monica. Our whole objective is to keep you away from them."

"Yeah, and how has that worked out so far? Sonechka is dead, we are prisoners in this condo, and someone tried to kill you already. You can't afford to take one of your operators off the table to babysit me. I *said* I'm going."

She might have a point, but... "No."

"No?"

Her face twitched, revealing a bit of surprise at my disagreement. But something had been bothering me since the start of this. She is a little too confident for her role as a hapless victim of violent men.

She's a liar.

She is holding out on us.

Liars and holdouts get people killed.

I closed in on her and let her see the set of my jaw. Monica needed to know what strained patience looked like. I wanted her to imagine what raising my ire might mean to her health.

I started slow, like warm water heating to a boil. "You know something, Monica. And whatever that 'something' is, they think you told us. That's why we're holed up here. That's why Sonechka is dead, and that's why Tiki and I were attacked today. Not because of our security measures. Whatever it is, they think you know more than a general description of who they are. Maybe it's time you tell us."

"I already told you, Becker." She lit a cigarette and tried to put me on ignore as she leaned back in her chair.

Everyone else in the place knows me pretty well. A line had been crossed. Their faces had the same expression as a guy in a war movie who just stepped on a landmine.

The pause in the discussion wasn't really as long as it seemed, but the room became very quiet, the vacuum of space quiet. I softly whispered my next words, widely spacing each spoken syllable, yet everyone could clearly hear me. "Give us the room,"

Nicolo tried to intervene. "Come on, Becker. She already..."

"Give us the room, now." I growled, no longer speaking quietly. The matter was no longer up for discussion.

My crew recognized the look. Nicolo, being an experienced cop, was quite familiar with a veteran cop's *you don't want to see what's going to happen next* face. I wasn't surprised that he tried to 'white knight' for Monica. But I think he has some of the same questions I do, questions that are better for me to ask than him. Nicolo was plenty tough, but he was never part of the goon squad, like me. He was neither a rule breaker nor a leg breaker. He's a decent person, an honest cop, a guy who colored inside the lines. I respect that, but our current situation required a firmer grip on the throat of reality. Polite society, if we are going to be honest, is for optimists and Canadians. It has no place in an investigation.

The room cleared.

Monica gave me a blank soulless stare through her stagnant pond eyes. No emotion, no fear, not a ripple of concern. "What you going to do, Becker. Get violent?"

She used the word violent like it was a commodity. Maybe it is.

"I'm going to get answers. You decide how." I wasn't going to get rough, but she needed to believe I would. I countered her impassiveness by pulling out a chair, sitting down, and lighting a cigarette of my own. I took a drag and stared back. No anger, no threat... When a woman digs her high heels into the carpet and jams the brakes, you don't push back... you let a quiet pause do its work, then shift gears to break their focus.

She was expecting violence. I wanted her not knowing what to expect at all.

I knew she'd break eye contact. It took a bit but eventually she mashed her cigarette butt into the ash tray and looked down.

I slowly reached into my suit coat, still giving her dead eye.

Her eyes widened. She didn't know me, but I suspect someone here told her about me. If so, she'd conclude that committing cold blooded murder wasn't a deal breaker for me. She also knew that me blowing a hole in her forehead would solve a lot of problems for everyone. Nico might not like it, but he'd get over it. Everyone would keep their mouths shut. At least, even if any of that was true or not, that's the realization I saw come over her face.

I didn't draw the Sig 220 from the holster under my coat. I pulled out a flask. I poured some in her coffee, and then took a long sip from it before returning to my coat pocket.

I gave the booze a moment to peregrinate its way through my bloodstream before I spoke. I was quiet but unyielding. "Knock off the bullshit, beautiful and give me what I need to save the fucking day. I'm not a mark, like your last boyfriend." My words were not delivered harshly or with anger, only direct, clear, and firm.

She smiled. Her posturing had run its course. Monica knew it was time to talk straight.

She took a sip of her upgraded coffee. "My last boyfriend? You say that like you might take his place." Monica gave me a sly smile that told me she would approve of that plan.

I smiled... then slowly drew my .45 out of the holster and placed it on the table. "Everything is on the table, Monica. Now talk."

My breaking the rhythm of the conversation again, or at least the way she saw it going, by escalating, de-escalating, and then ramping the tension up again, worked. She dropped the facade.

Her eyes gazed down at her hands and steadied rather than darting back and forth like a mouse in a cat lady's kitchen. The tightness in the corners of her mouth relaxed. She knew it was time for the truth.

"All right. I'm dead anyway if you don't stop them, Becker. What do you want to know?"

I felt mean... I guess I am mean. I needed to know a lot. The killing had already started. More killing won't change things now. "Everything... we start at the beginning, and you tell me everything... then, you play it straight with me until this is over or I will kill you myself... body in the swamp dead, because if you lie again, people I care about are in danger. Fair enough?"

"It works for me."

Then she told me a tale.

It wasn't what I expected to hear.

CHAPTER 6 - METAPHYSICAL MUSCLE

"The truth is harsh, Becker... and you'd be better off gathering your friends and getting them the hell out of Florida rather than hearing this."

"I don't leave Florida. I like a mojito once in a while and I find mosquitos to be charming... Now let's get real, lady. What's going on here?"

She started with some vague nonsense, like she was buying time to think. "Some new age gangsters."

"What?"

I hate new age gangsters. I don't even know what that means and I hate them.

"It's hard to explain. Have you heard of Professor Chen?"

"No."

"He's a third generation Chinese American."

"So?"

"He's a stock manipulator, extortionist, human trafficker, narcotics kingpin."

"So, he's a cop problem."

"No, that's not a cop problem. Cops don't even know he exists."

"Elaborate."

"I mentioned Professor Chen was a third

generation American."

"Yeah."

"But not on paper."

"Paper?"

"Yeah, his grandparents, his parents, the whole family operated without ever having any documentation. They entered illegally, kids were born at home without birth certificates, they operated with cash... all off the radar. When they needed something that required identification, they used fake papers or acquired stolen identities. There is no official record they exist here, yet they thrived and prospered by taking advantage of the system."

"So, it's a family?"

She frowned like she was getting to the serious part. "Not anymore. Chen was the most ruthless of his clan. Over the past twenty years, he killed every one of his family members and extended family members."

"That's insane."

"Being insane doesn't make it untrue."

I had to think about that one. I guess she has a point. Insanity isn't a disqualifier for reality anymore.

"So, if he is this stand-alone unknown foreign criminal, how does he operate?"

Monica explained. "He uses others. Sometimes street gangs and sometimes mobsters. He pays cash through his cut-outs, manipulates through extortion, and tells everyone he is a triad boss, sponsored by the communist party, which may be true. I don't know. He's nobody but he's everybody. Like a ghost"

I am often skeptical of paranormal crooks. These stories are almost always a product of imagination, fear, and jail-house fairy tales. But I wanted to hear more.

"I'm still lost here, who is doing the killing in Florida?"

"Chen has a small group working directly for him across the country, maybe five men... Guo is the most dangerous of them. He's the killer here in Florida."

"Is Conti dirty?"

"No, Luca never trusted him enough to tell him what he knew, but he didn't really suspect him of being the inside man either."

"Good to know."

"I wish I wasn't involved."

"Yeah, me neither, yet here we are. So, what's all this Chinese gangster stuff got to do with Nicolo? And how do you know all this?"

"Chen wants the casino. He wants more money laundering power and more influence in Florida. I know it because Luca told me everything. I didn't ask him. I didn't want this... but he told me. And the part about him using a speaker phone... that was true. Like I told you before, I heard most of Luca's business."

"You also told me this was a cartel thing."

"Yeah, I was lying... the cartel gets attention... I mean, let's face it, it got *your* attention. Some guy named Professor Chen not so much... I mean what level hood is named Professor Chen... a name like that and you imagine the worst thing he ever did was deduct points off your final exam for poor penmanship. Besides, at that point, I didn't know if I could trust you."

All that made sense. So, I focused on learning the Chen story. "How is Chen making moves?"

"Extorting and threatening board members. Letting everyone believe some mob syndicate in California was behind it, which was clever. He has a man inside the casino operation already embezzling funds and creating distrust within the board of directors. Luca figured it out. He was going to take what he had to the state cops."

"Why not the FBI?"

"Because he said they can't be trusted. Luca told me they are basically just 1920s era corrupt Chicago cops now. I don't even know what he meant by that. All I know about the FBI is Efrem Zimbalist Junior runs it."

"Yeah, but how did he catch on to Mister Invisible Kingpin? He's supposed to be invisible. Part of being invisible is people not catching on to you."

I really hate invisible metaphysical criminals. Especially foreign ones.

"Luca knew money, he knew criminals, and he had experience in raising capital in Hong Kong, Shanghai, and Singapore. He had a banker friend from Hong Kong who tipped him off. The banker and his family were all murdered. I guess he had Luca's phone tapped or something. Secrecy is more important to Chen than the casino. Chen tried to scare him into selling out... he ended up scaring him to death."

"So again, what's this got to do with Nicolo?"

"Luca told someone else on the board about going to the cops, I don't know who. That's what got him killed. That person ratted Luca out. Chen figured Luca probably told me, and I suppose he suspected I told Nicolo and Sonechka. Now they probably believe you and your people know, so you're on the hit list too."

"Oh."

I hate being on lists... especially hit lists.

She continued. "And Chen's policy is to instill fear, force cooperation, and kill everyone who resists or who could be a potential witness. Chen assigned Guo to hire some local muscle... the best, probably former Cuban special forces guys or local mob guys. They tried to kill me. They killed Luca and Sonechka. They tried to kill you. This is a losing proposition, Becker. All you can do now is run. Run like hell."

"Or kill Guo and Chen."

"You are not at their level, Becker. Guo will kill

you. He's like a devil. A big man. A vicious man."

"If I'm dead anyway, I might as well see if I can screw up Chen's day a little before I go." I lit another cigarette and took a puff. "If you can't have a little fun in this life, what's the point?"

She smiled, but I could feel the disdain crawling up my spine like a filthy bug. "The point is, all your friends will be dead. They might have a different opinion."

"We'll ask them. But first, a big question... is that big money stash you mentioned real?"

"Oh, it's real. Very real. I've seen it with my own eyes... and just so you know... Chen knows it exists... and he wants it too."

I called the crew back into the room. I could tell they expected I was going to cancel the operation. They shuffled in with all the enthusiasm of pro athletes reporting for a urine test.

I made Monica retell the story... this time she remembered a few more details like Chen having a full-floor penthouse condo in Miami and a black Rolls Royce. and Guo having a big scar on his face.

One might think a black Rolls is not the vehicle of choice for someone wanting to remain invisible, but one might not be from Miami either. Those are as common as Toyotas here.

When Monica finished, Joan spoke. "A murder spree...A ghost crime superman... So, now what? Do we quit?"

I flicked my Zippo and lit a smoke, followed by my rarely used but very popular evil grin. It was all the answer I needed to give.

Joan smiled. "We're going to kick some ass, aren't we."

I revised our plan and laid it out for everyone, who all seemed as happy as a squad of rookies with brand new ticket books and a radar gun.

Yeah. It was time to kick some ass.

I gave assignments.

"Nicolo, stay in disguise. We'll have you doing a recon while we set up down the street. Durd, can you set one of your drone things up on the target house?"

"I already have one on the target house. You should be able to get a feed on your phones now."

I should have known. Having a genius on the team has its benefits. We checked our phones and sure enough, there was a picture of the bad guy safe house Conti had told me about. He called them condos, but they were really one story adjoined places on an intra-coastal canal. There were eight units facing a long wooden dock. The bad guys were on the end. I noticed the street leading back to the condos was empty except for one car.

"Nicolo, do you see that car?"

"Yeah."

"Check it out."

"Copy that. Do you have a fishing pole here?"

Joan spoke, "I have a rig and tackle box in the

trunk of my car."

That surprised me for some reason. "You fish?"

She frowned, "Yeah, I'm an American. You don't?"

"Of course I do."

Nicolo interrupted the debate, "Joan, I'd like to use it as a prop to check out the dockside of the condos."

"You got it."

I finalized, "We take three cars. Nicolo, you run solo, Worm and Tiki, and I'll take Joan. I want her to be able to identify whatever is left of our friends after we visit. Durd, you run surveillance from here. We roll invisible but tactical."

"How about I take the van and tag along. I feel better being mobile."

"Good point. Uh, we have a van?"

Dourdhoff is full of surprises.

"*We* don't. I do… fully operational surveillance system. I designed it for DARPA but decided I needed one too. I need Worm to drop me off by my offices to pick it up."

"Do it. I'm not sure how long this place will stay off their radar anyway. No sense leaving you alone here. And also pull the sheet off of that ghost Chen and his goon, Guo."

"You got it."

The team dispersed to gather up gear for our little road trip to Miami.

An hour-and-a-half later I parked my Jaguar in a strip mall parking lot a mile from our target. The team was deployed and ready.

"Nicolo, go take a look. And check out that car."

"Copy that."

We watched from the drone camera as Nicolo ambled down the street with a pole and tackle box. Suddenly my screen divided, and I had a more angular shot paired with the overhead I'd been looking at. Dourdhoff came on the comm set he designed for us.

"I added a second drone hovering at a low angle behind Nicolo to give as a more ground-like view. You should have two video windows open on your screen."

Dourdhoff can be a handful, but the dude is a tech wizard. We could see very close to what Nicolo could see.

"Where did you find this Dourdhoff guy?" Monica asked, amazed at the level of tech that a private investigator had access to.

"Third grade."

"Oh." she decided not to pursue it.

Nicolo approached the car we thought might be driven by Conti's goons. I heard some rustling static and Nicolo's voice quivering out an 'oh shit.'

"What do you have?" I asked over my comm unit.

"Three dead guys. One shot to the forehead on

each of them."

Monica stiffened. Things got real again for her.

I asked, "Can you get a photo?" In the drone picture I could see him fish his phone out of a pants pocket and snap a shot.

Dourdhoff came on line, "I got the photo, sending now."

A photo of three dead guys came in a third window on my phone screen. Three dead guys.

Monica asked, "Do you know them?"

"Yeah, we've met." I said as I looked at the corpses of the guys who roughed me up at the casino... third or fourth string cannon fodder. What was Conti thinking by sending these rubes?

Nico came on the comm line, "The place is empty... not a sign of anyone ever being here."

"How did you get in?"

"Uh, magician."

"Oh..." For a moment I felt stupid for asking. Then I got over it and started giving orders. "Pick up Nicolo... We're going to look for Chen. Do you have an address on him yet, Durd?"

Dourdhoff spoke, "Maybe... he really is a ghost... almost... but I know who he is and where he is now... but not where his guys are staged."

"Send the address to everyone's phone."

"Done."

My curiosity was piqued. It didn't surprise me that Dourdhoff figured it out, but how he does it is a mystery. I gave a command. "We can't talk here.

Everyone, stage at the Galleria on Sunrise... Inside the parking garage."

We needed a regroup. This was getting weird.

CHAPTER 7 - CIRCLING THE WAGONS

I parked in a remote corner of the mall parking garage. I hadn't been here since the time I saw two guys who were robbing a lady accidentally fall and hit their heads. Accidents happen...

Within ten minutes the whole crew had circled the wagons, or in this case, our vehicles, and we started sorting out what was going on.

Dourdhoff spoke first. "I was able to access a doorbell camera across the street. We have the murder of the three casino guards on video. It was one guy, a big guy... scar on his face."

"Guo." I muttered.

"Very likely. But his real name is Ernest Miller. Guo was his mother's name. He is a war veteran who worked in OED, disarming and removing bombs and IEDs... not a special forces guy... still dangerous though."

From the corner of my eye, I saw Nicolo's jaw tighten at the mention of Guo being a bomb expert.

My theory on bomb experts is this... don't piss them off. Full stop.

Dourdhoff continued, "But Guo *is* a career criminal. He's been in and out of prison for the past twelve years." Dourdhoff paused, "He's not a nice person, Becker. He's a trained boxer and a sadistic bastard. He did one of his stretches for animal abuse, six months."

"Yeah, I don't like him," I lit a smoke. "What about his shit heel boss?"

"Chen is a fraud. Phony name and backstory. He's definitely wealthy, but he's a trust fund baby. His family is from Argentina... He has Chinese ancestry, but the whole 'ghost' thing is bullshit... except for murdering everyone in his family for sole control of the money part. He is a ruthless sicko... He's off the books here in the United States, but he is wanted in four other countries right now under various names for murder and extortion, he killed at least two people with a knife...he's like a villain in a spy movie except no volcano lair, just a condo in Miami."

'Evil Genius?" Vance asked.

"Not so much. More like just evil. His history doesn't indicate be who would in charge of an operation like a hostile take-over of a casino."

That didn't fit the narrative, but Chen had Nicolo's girl killed, so... Guo and Chen are off the Christmas card list and on the shit list.

"What's he look like?" Joan asked.

Dourdhoff described him. "Average height, average build, average face, black hair, brown eyes, and a cross of Asian and Hispanic. He dresses like a banker, or at least the way a banker used to dress.

From the one photograph of him I could find he has thick shoulders and upper body, maybe a gym rat."

Worm asked a question, "How many guys does he have?"

"Maybe twenty hard-core guys... and another dozen or so cannon fodder types from around Miami he is using for the casino take-over and other projects... not regulars, just local asswipes.

That made me smile. Durd is talking like a detective now, instead of using genius words all the time. There is hope for him yet.

He added, "And there are usually a few hotties hanging around. Chen likes the girls... a lot. Usually local high-end prostitutes, gold-diggers, and nightclub skanks."

Nightclub skanks? Yeah, he definitely sounds like an old school detective.

I summarized, "So, he is a wealthy secretive international criminal with a fake back story. He is a murderer who doesn't mind getting in close. He has a small army of goons and hookers. And he takes what he wants."

Dourdhoff nodded. "Yeah, that's about it."

I continued, "And Guo is a big muscle head who probably placed the bomb that killed Sonechka."

Dourdhoff's eyes narrowed. "Most likely, Becker. That is what I would deduce from this information."

Monica looked puzzled. "Dourdhoff, how did

you find this?"

Durd gave her a flat stare. "Have you heard of Interpol, the NSA, GRU, DGI, and the AFI?"

"Uh... I've heard of Interpol."

"Well, I designed all their software. Or at least a few of my companies did, I just did the main architecture on some of it. I always leave a back door."

"Really?"

Dourdhoff looked at her as if he found a turd in his lunchbox. "Miss, I do not exaggerate about technology."

Tiki snickered.

Monica decided not to push it. She just whispered, "Oh."

Rule of thumb, never piss off a guy who can hack the NSA.

Nicolo stood up and the look on his face caused any cheer in our immediate area to dive out a window to its death. He was grim, angry, and hurt.

"I want Guo."

I could see he wasn't thinking straight and didn't want to see him get a murder rap or worse on a revenge spree. "Nicolo... this is bigger than us... we need to go to the cops."

I was lying about the cops. Chen needs to be taken out, but it has to be done by someone who knows how to do it. Not a decent guy like Nicolo. Somebody like me.

Dourdhoff interrupted, "I don't think that is a

good idea, Becker."

"Why?"

"Chen is a federal informant."

"What?"

"The FBI bought into his phony China story. He has been stringing them along for years with a line of bullshit about the Chinese Communist Party. He owns the Bureau and they don't know it. He used them to indict one of his competitors in Los Angeles. They think he's the golden goose so they've been running interference for him forever, shutting down local police investigations."

"How do you know?"

"I know because the NSA and the Russians know."

"Why doesn't the NSA tell the Feebs?"

"The NSA plays the long game, Becker. They want to be the real core of the intelligence community. They hate the Bureau."

Nicolo piped in. "Everybody hates the Bureau."

I agreed but qualified the thought. "Yeah, but not on a peer-to-peer level. Those beltway guys are a special kind of ruthless."

Tiki asked, "What do you mean."

"Remember Snowden?"

"Yeah."

"There are rumors he was an FBI plant used to destroy NSA's reputation in Congress."

"That sounds like a crazy conspiracy theory."

"Yeah, it might be."

Durd concluded, "Yes, that might be a conspiracy theory, but the level of ruthlessness is quite true. And eventually, if the time is right, they will pull the rug out from under the Bureau with some public humiliation, whether it be payback or just gamesmanship."

Monica was a bit overwhelmed with our data dump and speculation. "Seriously? What makes you say that, Durd?"

"The Deputy Director of the NSA Operational Directorate is a friend from M.I.T."

Monica asked, "So, you were classmates?"

"No, he attended an elective course I was teaching on the Stothers, Vassilevska-Williams and Le Gall enhancements to the Coppersmith and Winograd algorithm. As it turned out, the Deputy Director happens to be a watch collector too. We have lunch once in a while. His name is Harry... but that is probably an alias. He's a spy chief. He wears an Omega at official functions... which is droll."

She gave another humbled, "Oh."

The confusion on the face of a non-collector about such an important observation was to be expected.

Durd rambled on. "Yeah, I know he has a Patek Philippe Calatrava... crazy, huh? It's so much more classy. But he has to go for that secret agent look in public events... such a nerd."

I felt a little sorry for Monica's first exposure to the patented Dourdhoff over-explanation syndrome. I guess it wouldn't be so bad if normal humans had a clue as to what he was talking about.

I lit up a Lucky Strike and took a long drag and felt a deep thought bounce around in my head. *What the hell is our next move?*

The group became quiet now. Nicolo was seething, Dourdhoff was computing with a little device that he was whispering data into, Vance was leaning on a car fender writing stuff down, Tiki was watching the area like a sentry, Monica was scratching her head, and Worm was surreptitiously scratching his groin, except it wasn't that surreptitious.

I had to make a call on this... in or out. Get revenge or be a good citizen and call the cops. Or maybe it's simpler than that... kill him before he kills us.

This is why I miss working alone.

I switched gears. "I need to call Conti. Let him know his men are dead. You guys sort out our options."

Walking away from the group, I dialed Conti's private number at the casino. He picked up on the first ring and started talking.

"Becker, I think our problem is taken care of. I sent some guys."

"Yeah, about that."

"What?"

"You need to pick up three bodies. Your boys got

whacked."

"What?" Cool cat Conti was now sounding a bit alarmed.

"Yeah, they're dead."

"How?"

I gave him a brief rundown on what we discovered. Not the whole thing, but enough to scare the hell out of him.

I heard a deep sigh that sounded a lot like a guy who wasn't used to being in over his head.

I continued with some specific tasks. "Tell Gilheaney, your security chief, to head over there now... just scoot the driver over and drive out. And tell him to bring some plastic to sit on, the seat is a little gooey."

"Ewww."

"Yeah."

Conti made a weird noise like he was choking back a puke... a moment later he composed himself and asked, "Then what?"

"Gilheaney will know what to do. I suspect a car crash into a pond full of hungry gators is in their future."

"What the hell is going on, Becker?"

"You might want to stay at the casino and triple your personal security until this is over. Have Gilheaney hand pick the guys. I'm going to dissuade our little thorn in the side Chen to seek greener pastures."

"Chen?"

"Yeah, I think he's calling the shots."

"But what do you mean? What kind of pastures?"

"A very small plot of land in a quiet area."

"Oh... so, no cops?"

"Right... no cops. Tell Gilheaney I need to meet him when he is done with the bodies. Tell him to come alone. We'll need another gun."

"I thought you said you weren't a bodyguard or hitman."

"That's right. I'm not... I'm something worse."

I disconnected and walked back to the crew. They were arguing points and testing theories against each other. That told me they didn't have a plan yet either.

The worst thing about being in charge is sometimes you don't know what to do. Every option is based on chance, random events, unpredictable behavior. Every choice could be a bad one... in fact, most of the choices will probably be bad ones.

But I like it that way. It's why I joined the cops. I wanted chaos...not routine. Some people are just wired this way. They call us lunatics.

So, when in doubt, take a nap, drink, or have a cup of coffee... eventually an idea will percolate to the top of that muddled garbage heap of life.

I walked back to the circle of vehicles with the rest of the crew... we'd been in 'catnapping only' mode for two days. Everyone looked tired.

I spotted two yawns and a pair of watery red eyes. When you are tired, mistakes are made. I decided my former career criminal butler and my computer nerd pal had the most gas in the tank. Either one of them could run for a week on pop-tarts and energy drinks. The rest of us needed to downshift into a real break.

"Durd, you and Worm set a remote surveillance on Chen's condo. Try to pick up the trail again if they leave. Take turns getting some rest. Vance and Tiki, go to the casino and make sure Conti is tucked in. He's our prime defense witness if we get dragged into court for whatever comes next. As soon as you get Conti tucked in take a break. Get a hotel, hide, sleep."

Durd, do you have fake IDs and credit cards in the van?"

"Yeah."

"Good. Set all of us up to get rooms across the city under fake names. We need a few hours of rest. Stay under wraps until I get a location, then we put the bag on Guo and Chen.

Nicolo bristled, "They're mine, Becker."

I put my hand on his should and looked him in the eye. "If we can arrange that we will. But first we have to survive." I tried to end that discussion by addressing everyone. "We'll rest in shifts."

Nicolo wasn't having it. "I'll stay with Dourdhoff and Mister Worm. I already slept. If I get tired, I'll sleep in the van."

"Fine but don't get so exhausted you do something stupider than usual."

"Copy that."

It was as much cooperation as I could hope to get out of him. But the kind of internal rage he's feeling doesn't stay bottled up forever.

Monica spoke, "I'll go with you, Becker. I haven't really slept since this started. I was too freaked out at the condo."

"Fine, I'll get us each a room at the Conrad."

Durd provided everyone with an ID and an active but untraceable matching credit card loaded with a ten-thousand-dollar limit. We all split up for our assignments.

The drive to the Conrad was a short one. I went to the reception desk and booked two adjoining rooms on the second floor. One level up from the lobby was a survivable jump if we had to leave in a hurry. Security officers were routinely posted by the elevator to make sure only the guests had access to rooms. This place was as safe as we were going to get and still be in town.

Exhaustion began curling up in my brain like a sleepy cat. I hadn't fallen asleep more than ten minutes at a time since this started. Well, maybe once, but I'm old and need more sleep than the rest of these clowns. Sometimes I sleep and then forget I slept. It's complicated.

We walked together to the rooms. I stuck my card in my door and opened it. I started to go in.

Monica slipped through the door ahead of me. I stepped in behind her and closed the door.

"You should go to your room, Monica. I need to get some rest. You'll be safe."

"I can't be alone right now, Becker. I have to relax... I have to feel safe. I can't be alone and feel safe."

She walked by me and into the bathroom. I heard the shower switch on... she didn't close the bathroom door.

What the hell is going on here?

Only because I am an expert trained observer did I notice her naked body through the steam. She opened the glass doors on the bath and hand signaled me to join her.

Every professional fiber of my being told me to go close the bathroom door and ignore her... There was no good outcome to following her invitation. But my hormones told me otherwise. I might be old, I might be a little overweight, I might be kind of homely... but I'm not dead. I justified my next move by lying to myself... this is normal, and I should just go with it.

I stepped into the spacious bathroom... like an idiot.

She pressed her body against the glass and slowly gyrated, first the back, with her soft round bottom, and then the front, slowing rubbing her breasts against the glass... she was being playful, making an invitation... it was sexy... and even though I am rarely effected by such displays, my free will escaped the coils of personal and professional discipline.

She peeked out. My physical reaction to her seduction was no secret. I looked like I had a missile in my pants. It made her giggle... approvingly... dammit!

Powers outside my control somehow caused all my clothes to fall off. This mysterious force undid my tie, kicked off my shoes, undid my trousers, unbuttoned my shirt, and the next thing I knew I was happily nude and entering the shower. Totally not my fault.

I hungrily grabbed her, pressed her body between the shower wall and me, lifting her... I felt her legs squeeze around my waist... her mouth locked on mine, and we kissed deeply, hard, desperately...

Four hours later I awoke from a deep sleep. Maybe the deepest sleep I have had since that crazy night in the hot tub with... never mind, I need to forget her. She dumped me so I broke up with her.

Room service had delivered coffee. Evidently Monica had our clothes cleaned and pressed while I was out. I wouldn't have been surprised to find she had cleaned my 45. This was a woman who knew things about men.

Of course, the old '*what the hell did I just do?*' thought tried to crash my mood, but this time I ignored it. I didn't realize how much I needed this.

Monica was sitting in a chair across the room, naked and sipping coffee.

"Hi sleepy head," she chirped as beautifully as a little songbird that just gobbled a fresh grub out of a dead tree.

"Hi, yourself." I didn't have a snappy answer. I felt a little dumb... But I felt young again...I liked the feeling. I don't let my guard down often. Maybe I should reconsider that policy.

"You received a text from Vance... sorry, I saw it on your phone. We're meeting in two hours... they have something."

"Two hours?"

"Yeah... two hours..."

She stood and did a slow erotic walk toward me in a sleek animalistic move that might have been invented by Sally Rand.

Common sense was still out to lunch, so my libido kicked in again... not bad for an old-timer.

Monica curled in beside me... one hundred and ten minutes later I was dressed for work.

We didn't say much on the drive to the meeting place. I preferred to exercise my right to remain silent. I just committed a serious faux pas in the small and dirty world of detectives... never boink a client and absolutely never boink a victim... and although I told myself she wasn't technically the client, I knew better. She might not be writing the check but she's a client... and she was the victim in a missing person case.

What the hell is wrong with me?

I glanced down at my lap to give the true guilty party in this sad affair a dirty look.

What the hell is wrong with you?

My weiner didn't respond... evidently, he doesn't consider himself to be a detective and isn't held by the same standard the rest of me is.

Bastard!

Monica didn't seem bothered by any guilt or remorse. I wish I could be like that. My typical inner dialogue is ninety-percent guilt and remorse... it comes with a police career.

Monica spoke without looking at me.

"That was fun, Becker. I needed that."

I didn't know what to say. I decided to stick with simple agreement. "Yeah... me too."

It was difficult to determine with any certainty, but I felt like she considered the experience strictly recreational. That was fine with me. But if she said let's go another round, I would have whipped a bat-turn back to the hotel and gone for it... Apparently, I have the moral fiber of a motherless goat... and what the hell is a motherless goat? Where did that random thought come from? Is that from a movie?

I'm losing my mind. Focus Becker, people are trying to kill your horny ass.

My current internal self-talk ended as we rolled up to the meeting place, a small park on the intra-coastal. We gathered at a table and jump started our case.

Tiki, a former professional sex-worker, gave me a funny look. She sees through anything that might be remotely intimate. It's creepy.

Does she know?

Fortunately, she didn't say anything. She and Monica seemed refreshed and cleaned up. I guess they took their break. The guys had obviously been taking turns sleeping in the van. It was wise to hold this meeting outdoors. They were a little ripe.

Being the leader, I started the briefing, "Where are we on this?"

Vance, being the informal leader, or at least the more responsible entity in the Becker Investigations management team, led it off. "The shooters are in the wind. They didn't go back to the condo we think Chen is in. But there is activity at Chen's place."

I put it to the crew, "We need their location. That's our last lead. We need that location now." Then I remembered something. "Durd, can the money tell us anything? Did we hear from Rochester Billington? Maybe if we figure out the money trail, we can get a location."

"He might have something. You were going to call him, right?"

I didn't want to talk to Rochester and get humiliated about not being old money, not that I care. But I needed information. When you need information, you make the uncomfortable calls. I walked away from the others for some privacy.

A few seconds later Rochester came on line. "So good to hear from you, old man. What sort of thuggery do you have yourself involved in this time?"

Thuggery?

I started with a lie, "Good to talk to you again, Rocky."

He hates being called Rocky.

I heard a snort on the other side of the conversation.

I continued with my beg. "I'm playing a game of pin the tail on the kingpin. Somebody is dirty at the casino."

"Yes, Dourdhoff, the old rascal, sent that file to me."

"Yes, he is a rascal. But someone on the board is working with a Chinese organized crime guy... I think. I need to know who is really in charge."

"I've reviewed your work. Your dossier is quite thorough actually, for someone who doesn't understand finance, business, or money in general. Quite thorough, indeed. Not quite professional by any means, but thorough."

Lord, please kill me now.

I get so sick of his curve ball insults. He thinks he's better than everybody... and maybe he is. But, he's my pal and even if I hate his guts, we are friends. What can one do?

He continued, "I can't say specifically..."

That asshole just called me by my first name.

"...but I think the board is clean. That's why they can't find the problem. You have an agent provocateur in the mix. Someone near the top. And Chen might be some form of local riff-raff, but a sophisticated thug he is not, in spite of his flamboyant style and his obscene group of miscreants and ruffians. He is merely someone playing rich who is not of true money, like you, somewhat, but not really."

I don't even know how to respond to that.

"Fine, thanks, Rocky... tell the boys at the club that Becker said huzzah."

I'm not sure what huzzah means, but rich people say it... and I'm a multi-millionaire... and why am I taking guff off this silver spoon knob? Maybe because multi-millionaires are nothing in the scheme of old money?

Billington money-snorted at my huzzah. "Do you want me to make a call, Becker?"

"To who?"

"Someone who can help you with this puzzling dilemma."

"No, I'm good. Thanks, Rochester..." *You condescending dick.*

"Well, please put a time in the old appointment book to come up and do lunch. My colleagues here love a good detective story... or whatever it is you call yourself now... detective... policeman... security guard... all quite entertaining. Just be sure to dress appropriately should you deign to visit your old chum."

"I can't wait to meet them all. Thanks..." *I puked a little in my mind... also my mouth.*

"Good day, old bean."

He said that intentionally. Nobody says old bean anymore unless they just purchased Boardwalk while wearing a top hat and monocle.

I secured all my inexplicable wealth anxiety and walked back to the crew. Rochester can be exhausting but the rich bastard is seldom wrong. Never underestimate someone who thinks they are better than you, just in case they might be better than you.

At least now I have a starting point and a germ of a plan. It was time to count the tally.

Obviously, things are not as they seem. It doesn't appear to be a board member selling the casino out... and Chen might not be the main guy behind all of it. Chen might simply be hired muscle with an inflated reputation. That doesn't leave me much to go on. But even if Chen is a low-level conspirator, he tried to have me kidnapped, probably killed Sonechka, and murdered my three sparring partners from the casino. Those dead casino goons might have been stupid, and they might have been losers, but they were just doing their job. They needed an ass-beating and strict supervision, not murdered. So, it's time to put the bag on Chen. I never liked him anyway.

I shared the information I received from Rochester with Vance and Durd... but I did it privately. No one else needs to know the direction this is taking yet. Maybe Tiki does, but the truth is, she doesn't care that much about information. Tiki is in it for the action, not the intrigue.

It was time to roll up Chen and find out what he's up to.

CHAPTER 8 - TWIST
THE KNOB

"Here's how it will go," I explained. "We set up on Chen's place and wait. According to Durd's surveillance, he moves every afternoon around two and goes to the Vista Cafe on Federal Highway. We will put the bag on him in the parking lot."

So far, the plan didn't seem to cause anyone any heartburn, so I continued. "We take him to a storage locker on NW Sixth Street. Then we have a talk."

Durd asked, "What about his security detail?"

"We rough them up, but we don't kill anybody. Shock and awe."

Tiki spoke up, "I have a better idea."

"I'm listening."

"Let me go to condo and get him, bring him out to the street and then you take him to the warehouse."

"How?"

"Durd told us before… Chen like the nightclub skank."

"Yeah." I still didn't get her point.

Tiki was extremely enthusiastic about her idea and so the pigeon english started kicking in. "You drop me off in limo. I go in be nightclub skank, convince him I have a score in car outside. He come out to look, you put on bag."

"What if he sends Guo instead?" Worm asked.

"We take Guo... just as good. He probably know plenty." Tiki answered.

Vance was skeptical. "Do you think a mobster at that level will come out to a car to look at a score over a hot chick?"

Tiki took the question as a challenge, if not a direct insult, and her diction sank further. "He mobster. Smart about mob. Stupid about girl. Stupid about score. I tell him I have bunch of diamonds from East Flagler in jewelry district."

Durd was impressed, "She might be right, Becker. It would be a lot less messy than fighting his goons at the cafe."

Nicolo spoke out, "If you all can give me two hours, and if Tiki gets him to the street, I can make it work. No one will get hurt."

"How?"

"Magic."

"Uh... but won't..."

Nicolo ignored me. "Don't worry about it... but I need some diamonds... they can't look fake."

Durd offered, "I have a few coffee cans full of diamonds in the vault you can use. But they're real."

Nicolo's eyes widened. He wasn't used to working with high-net-worth individuals. "Uh, sure... great. I'll make sure you get them back."

"Meh." Durd went back to messing around with his computer.

"I also need a few props from my stuff. I keep a lot of it in my storage locker."

Worm eagerly answered the request, "I'll pick them up for you."

The team was really getting into the spirit of whatever the hell this is.

"I'll make you a list. It's all labeled, you should be able to find it easily. I'll need a limo, make that two limos, a big mirror, and some air horns, the hand-held ones like on a boat. And I need everything in place at one-thirty."

I was very confused. "So, what are we doing?"

"We're making a mobster disappear and we're making him cooperative in one fell swoop."

Whenever someone says, 'one fell swoop' I always think of 'one swell poop.' I guess I'm juvenile that way. I successfully fought the urge to say it out loud, because I'm mature.

The team was chattering about the gig, but I noticed Monica was off to the side, she seemed isolated and withdrawn. I joined her, "What's up?"

"I'd like to go back to the room. I can't handle any more violence."

Was that a tear forming under her eye?

"I understand, Monica... I'll get a ride-share to pick you up. I'll come by when this is done."

"Thanks, Becker..." she gave me a hug then I

rejoined the crew.

An animated Tiki asked something about four gallons of fake blood being enough. Durd and Worm were working on a timetable and some hand signals. Nicolo was giving orders and answering questions. All was proceeding as planned... mostly... except the plan part. I'm not sure this could be legally called a plan.

Two hours later, Tiki made her move.

I sat back in the reclined driver's seat of my Jaguar, parked down the street from the condo, watching... just watching. My company is running a complex operation with a nerd, ex-hooker, an ex-criminal, a magician, and a Los Angeles transplant cop... and for the first time, I didn't have a direct role in it. I felt old. Hopefully, I'd be able to beat some information out of Chen later, or maybe knife him... you know, in the interests of elevating my mood and feeling like part of the team again. I mean, I really wouldn't enjoy hurting him that much, necessarily... it a would be for a team building thing. I mean, I wouldn't mind ending that turd, but that wouldn't be the main purpose if I did. You see, as we grow older, we all have to find our ever-evolving role in society and our social circles... even if it means stupid stuff like patiently waiting to punch someone later, rather than being the guy who goes through the door first blazing away with a gun. Maybe that's the meaning of maturity. You don't always have to be the first one to shoot a guy in the face all the time. You can be just as much a part of the team by simply beating the crap out someone later, like an elder statesman would do. I must learn the patience and the gravitas of my role. But either way, Chen wasn't getting out of this shit alive.

I noticed the limo pulling up and began focusing on the job at hand, rather than pondering the meaning of the universe. Worm was behind the wheel, dressed like a standard issue limo driver who has unkempt red hair sticking out the sides of his hat. Other than the hair, he looked the part.

Tiki exited the back of the big car and released a level of sexy onto the world that made my lap hurt, which was creepy because she's my friend. A very, very, very short yellow sun dress with extensive cleavage exposure adorned her svelte but curvy frame. She had a wide-brimmed black lady's hat with a splash of lace that matched her lace underpants, which everyone could see as she somewhat brazenly stepped up and onto the sidewalk. She carried a small Prada purse, that I knew contained her sample of the loot to show to Chen, a small bag of diamonds.

The street-side sidewalk was wide, and the distance from car door to condo door was almost twenty yards, with a private fenced lawn featuring a brick walkway that wound through the dense tropical landscaping, to the door. Raised winding concrete curbing held back the artificial jungle, preventing it from spreading and turning the entire block back to nature.

She wiggled her steaming hot body from the car all the way to the condominium entrance, delighting a couple of Chen's torpedoes who were standing guard outside the tall wooden double doors, smoking cigarettes, and watching the street. One of them even opened the door for her.

Durd was in the delivery truck across the street. I had an air horn… None of this made sense.

Ten minutes later, as she predicted, she was on the street with Chen.

Tiki Cha Cha… irresistible… dangerous… smart… sexy, bagged her man. Operatives like that are a gift from the Titans… or somebody… I don't recall what Titans are to tell you the truth, but like highly skilled undercover detectives, they are rare.

I switched on my monitor and watched the happenings inside of the limo like I was watching a movie. Our limo had a pair of wide-angle hidden cameras and at least three high quality microphones that were capturing everything that happened.

Tiki slid into the seat beside an unconscious man in a suit with a briefcase chained to his arm. The man had a long beard and hair and the black clothing, a stereotypical diamond merchant…if you don't really know anything about diamond merchants. Yeah, we leveraged a stereotype to pull a con.

The unconscious man was slouched in the seat.

Tiki crawled over him on all fours holding up a long handcuff chain that was attached to the briefcase and the unconscious man's arm. She grabbed the briefcase and showed it to Chen like she was revealing the grand prize on a game show.

"Lookie this, Chen. Big money!"

Her voice came across like a savvy prostitute who never mastered much English. It was good. It made me wonder if she had always been acting when she laid on the accent around me.

She chattered away, "Chain on diamond guy... This case full of diamonds... Give me twenty grand I give it to you... maybe worth a million... you make out good on this."

I could see Chen, now almost fully in the car with her, rapidly darting his eyes from Tiki's butt to the briefcase, to the man. He was confused, excited, horny, and greedy all at the same time. Even for an experienced criminal, this might have been sensory overload.

"Fine, bring in the case, and we have a deal."

Tiki responded by saying, "Deal." Then she reached under the seat, pulled out a big knife and cut the man's arm off at the wrist.

Chen, a man as tough as they come on the streets, screamed like a little girl who just found a squirming green lizard in her dollhouse.

Tiki looked at him like a bully looks at a scrawny kid's lunch money. "What wrong with you, Chen? You afraid of little blood? Here." She handed him the knife before he could mentally process the smart move of refusing to take it.

At that moment, the man sat up and screamed in agony. Chen smacked his head on the car roof as he jumped back in shock hard enough to stun him.

Tiki shouted. "He not dead enough!" She grabbed Chen's wrist and jammed the knife in the diamond merchant's chest while it was still clasped in Chen's hand. The man slumped back, now motionless. Blood spattered everywhere... it was disgusting... but cool.

Chen's men started slow walking toward the car as they must have heard the commotion.

Then things got weird.

Worm reached around, popped Chen on the head with a ball peen hammer, Tiki pulled Chen the rest of the way into the car, slammed the door, duct taped Chen's mouth and zip tied his hands and feet. I'm not sure if she learned that from Vance or if that was a service she sold back in her hooker days.

Then, something I didn't expect happened. It wasn't that I didn't know a truck would come by, because that was my cue to blast the air horn. What surprised me was my pal Tommy from Lauderdale was driving, and a lean woman who looked like she should be fronting a metal band was standing in the back of a glass delivery truck. The truck had big racks on the sides holding various sheets of what might be plexiglass or sheet glass covered in canvas. I couldn't see clearly what they were doing but I knew my signal was coming to blast the horn. I jammed my foam ear protectors into my ears.

The guards were crossing the twenty-yard gap from the door to the curb. Worm started the limo. The glass truck was moving.

What happened next should have never worked. But I admit, I don't understand the psychology of magic. I stuck both hands out the window, a nautical air horn in each paw, and let both horns let rip with a ten second blast.

Loud?

Oh yeah, very loud.

The hoods looked my way, confused.

The glass truck then blasted its astonishingly loud horn as it passed them. Simultaneously, the woman in the back of the truck pulled a canvas protective sheet off a shower door sized mirror, capturing the full reflection of the afternoon sun and redirecting it straight into the eyes of the two goons. It was arc welder bright and hit them like a laser weapon. I was surprised they didn't melt.

The piercing noise and unexpected bright light disrupted and overloaded their goon nervous systems and wrecked all of their higher-order perception functions. They covered their eyes and turned away.

Worm tossed a fast-deploying smoke grenade out the window, the same device that Nicolo used on stage in his disappearing alligator trick. The immediate area of the car was instantly consumed in a dark gray smoke.

At that moment, the limo pulled away, and Vance drove up in an identical limo, left it running at the curb as she dashed out, used an oven mitt to snatch up the smoke grenade, and jumped into the back of the glass truck. Worm drove the limo a hundred feet away and immediately pulled into the underground garage of an adjoining building.

While this commotion was going on, Durd approached on foot from the opposite side of the condo building and yelled, "Knock it off, you assholes!" Then he disappeared back around the side, but he did momentarily capture the attention of the somewhat blinded and deafened security men, long enough to fully execute the limo switch.

To an unaware outsider, one might have thought two random vehicles, the truck and the limo, were road raging with their horns, and a concerned citizen on foot joined in the fun. But for the two security guards, the limo containing the driver, their boss, and the hot chick was still there... and the limo's occupants had vanished into the netherworld.

It was rough around the edges as far as magic goes, but it worked. I participated in a magic trick, something I never expected would happen.

We disappeared ourselves and moved on to phase two.

Now I suppose these two tough, but not particularly smart guards, will soon be somewhere explaining to Guo how their boss Chen disappeared before their very eyes.

In the parking structure next door, Tiki and Worm pulled Chen out of the limo and stuffed him into the trunk of a rented sedan. Nicolo got out of his jewel merchant outfit, stuffing his disguise, the fake arm, and the trick knife in a canvas bag, and joined the team in the rental car.

"Anybody want a cool fake beard?" he asked as he held his faux whiskers out at arm's length.

"Not today, pal" Tiki snickered. "That was fun though!"

Worm agreed, "Yeah, let's do that again."

Nicolo smiled for the first time in a while, "Good job! You two can join the act anytime."

I'd send a tow truck later to pick up the abandoned curbside limo and Worm could recover the limousine from the parking garage later. We all met at the designated warehouse in twenty minutes.

We left Chen in the trunk to stew while we debriefed.

Vance introduced us to the additional crew, "Everyone, this is June Glume, a private detective and former cop from San Diego. She is who we had Tommy from Lauderdale working with on that security gig I told you about. When I told June that a retired cop's girl was a murder victim, she volunteered to help."

Glume shook hands with everyone. "Yeah, that's a no brainer. We can't tolerate that anywhere. I might not be a cop anymore, but my blood runs PD blue. I'm just glad I could help."

Tommy spoke up, "It definitely made our day more interesting. I'm no cop but I hate assholes. When this thing is over, beers for everyone at the restaurant are on me."

Nicolo, feeling the true love in the brotherhood of blue, might have had some unintentional moisture in his eyes as he addressed Glume. "Thank you, June. I appreciate what you did." Nicolo reached to shake hands with June but she gave him a hug.

"Anytime, brother. We can't ever make this right, but we can make them pay."

I suddenly felt a little moisture in my right eye… allergy season I suppose.

Tommy looked at his watch, "We got to jet. June and I have another business meeting in half an hour." We all said our goodbyes and Tommy and June left to return to her job.

The group aimlessly shuffled around a moment, everyone wondering if they should say the standard 'she's nice' comments but saying nothing. June was nice, but she seemed like she might be capable of cutting your throat if you crossed her. Enough said. Our minds were back on the case.

Durd scratched his head, "I can't believe that even worked."

Nicolo gave us a quick magic lecture. "As I've told some of you before, there are ten steps in magic, my friends. It's not that complicated, and it doesn't have to be particularly polished to work. We used the techniques of vanishing, production, transformation, transposition, restoration, escape, and prediction in this one... leveraging showmanship, acting, misdirection, and timing as we convinced two men that what they saw was what we wanted them to see, what their mind told them to see. The unique circumstances we created out there enabled the guards to believe that three people simply disappeared off the face of the earth. Nothing else made sense to them, even though we were rushed and unrehearsed in our delivery."

Tiki joined in, "I liked the fake knife and cutting off the arm."

Nicolo nodded. "That's very basic magic. Disguise and misdirection sold the diamond story to Chen. We used his lust and greed against him as weapons. And you were very convincing as a nasty cold-blooded murderer."

Tiki curtsied. "Thank you."

Worm smiled at her admiringly.

I smiled too at the next funny piece of news I had to share. "For our personal and professional entertainment, Durd has produced a video, with a few untraceable edits, that depicts Chen murdering a diamond merchant in the back of the limo. I don't know how he did it, but it looks very real. We have leverage for our forthcoming conversation."

Worm suddenly seemed a bit concerned and also a bit behind the curve, "So we just did that... thing... with tricks and stuff, but not *real* magic like a witch or a monster would use, right?"

Vance looked at him crookedly, "Are you asking or just saying?"

Nicolo responded in deadpan, "It's a legitimate question... however, it is a question that under the code of magicians, I can never fully answer." Nicolo gave his man of mystery look as he said it.

Worm looked a bit worried and whispered under his breath. "Oh shit." He did a quick sign of the cross.

Tiki eye-rolled him. Durd started to chuckle, then creeped out, then tried to chuckle again to cover his creeping out.

I don't know how Nicolo pulled it off, but he bought us some time while Chen's gun thugs sort out what the hell just happened to them. It was now time to get the information we needed. "Let's get to work on Chen."

I popped the trunk and Nicolo gently grabbed Chen by the lapels, carefully tossing him from the trunk to the concrete floor, where his head made a 'thonk' sound when he landed. I'm going to go out on a limb here and call that a totally accidental concussion.

We sat him up in a corner. Durd gave him a shot of adrenaline in the thigh... I don't know where he got the drug or why he had it, but the needle full of energy juice worked. Chen was wide awake and alert.

I started our conversation by slapping his face until my hand was sore on both sides. He deserved the paint brushing I gave him, and I didn't mind doing it. Then we got to the meat and potatoes of the discussion. "Who ordered the hit on Sonechka?

"Who?"

"The magician's girl."

"Who?"

"The casino... the magician."

"I know nothing."

It appeared he didn't really understand the serious nature of our investigation. I decided to up the stakes and pointed out Nicolo. "This is Sonechka's boyfriend. They were in love. You murdered Sonechka. He has a chain saw. You work out how this is going to go."

We didn't really have a chain saw, but it would have been a nice touch. Nevertheless, Chen decided to be a responsible citizen and spill his guts. I was disappointed. I was hoping this scumbag would be a little tougher. We didn't even get to extort him with our video.

"Wait. Wait.Wait..." he sputtered, "It wasn't me.

It was Guo… He did the killings… Not me."

"Did you order it?"

"No… yes… but I was getting orders… this is not my idea… I'm just a contractor, not my deal. I don't know anything about the casino."

Vance interjected. "What about the mobsters from California?"

"Who?"

"The gangsters… Mafia… Oceanside, California."

"They work for somebody else… we're all taking our orders from the casino… the insider… not our deal… we get paid on the backend…"

It was my turn to be confused. "You mean you are just some dipshit hired muscle?"

"Yes… I'm a dipshit… Please, don't kill me."

Nicolo got in on the interrogation fun. He marched over and stood Chen up and held him against the wall. "Did you give the order to bomb the car at the casino?"

"Only because I was told to get rid of loose ends."

"So, you did."

"Yeah, but I didn't mean anything by it, man. It was just a job."

I forgot Nicolo had a gun, so you can imagine my surprise when he pulled the Glock from his waistband, jammed the barrel down Chen's pants, and pulled the trigger four times.

The screaming was louder than the usual screaming you hear nowadays. Chen was screaming, Nicolo was screaming, I might have screamed a little. Let's be candid, we were all surprised by Nicolo's violent outburst... but he's a traffic cop and this is just how they are... kind of insensitive.

"Nicolo," I shouted over the ringing in my ears, "You shot him in the nuts."

"I wasn't done. The gun jammed. I was going to blow his head off too."

At that point, I heard Worm and Vance duet an 'Aww shit,' and I noticed what might have been a gaping hole in the area of Chen's femoral artery. I blubbered an 'Awww Shit' too.

Pushing Nicolo out of the way I shook Chen and asked him, "Give me the boss's name.... who is behind this?"

He gave me a look like drunk drivers do when you ask them to recite the alphabet... Confused, and a bit surprised they can't do it.

I knew we were screwed.

No name - No case.

And just like that, Professor Chen, died like a dirty dog on the concrete floor. I guess now when someone refers to him as a ghost, it will be a more accurate description.

I heard Mister Worm's voice announce, "I'll find a mop."

It's good to have a butler. Later I'd have him feed the local alligators, not Worm, I mean Chen... but for now, we had one thread left to tug... Mister

Guo.

Four hours later we all gathered at the safe house. I tried to call Monica, but she wasn't answering. The front desk at the Conrad said she checked out. She probably got smart and caught a flight to Rio.

Vance, Tiki, Durd, Nicolo, and I were all in the thinking mode, processing what happened and what to do next. Worm was still out somewhere, presumably the local Everglades, serving Chenburgers to the gators. I hope they like Chinese delivery.

My frustration was high... I wanted to close this thing out quietly... yet here we are, disposing of bodies, not having any sort of a plan, and our only lead is a monster-sized street enforcer with a scar on his face and very few interpersonal skills supplemented with a herd of street hoods who are protecting him as he assumes Chen's old job.

I drew a line in the sand. "I'm going to get Guo... I'll question him. And FYI, I might try to get some answers before someone takes it upon himself to mag-dump our suspect's nuts next time." I peered accusingly at Nicolo.

He shrugged. "You know, that was mostly an accident if you think about it."

Listening to this kind of bullshit is why my hair is mostly gone.

Vance the pragmatic among us changed the subject and asked an appropriate question. "How are we going to get Guo? They will be expecting us."

I decided to keep it simple. "Not we... I... I'm going to drive over to the condo, beat his ass, and make him talk."

Vance wasn't on board. "Boss, he's a tough one... maybe we need to wait for Worm and maybe hire the defensive line of the Dolphins."

"I can handle him. I've handled assholes like him my entire life." I could hear my Irish temper whispering in my ear, *'yeah, beat his ass... the sooner the better.'*

"I know you have Becker, but you've had a whole bunch of entire life. Geo is maybe thirty and hitting his prime. And he is a monster... and did you forget about the twenty or thirty guys?"

"They can't *all* be tough."

Vance didn't quit. "Uh, yeah, they can be. That's probably the qualification that got them hired."

"Look, I'm tired of messing around. If you feel like I'm too old and feeble to do my job, just say so."

I suspected now that my frustration and chronic inner rage were controlling my thinking. But I was still mad. So why am I arguing with Vance? She's the best thing that ever happened to my business, and a close friend. I respect her... and she might be right.

Tiki jumped in, "We all go. I want to see Becker beat down some bad guys."

I don't think I'm going alone now. I am defeated. I

know it. They know it.

"Fine. We all go. But I'm leading this raid."

Durd interrupted, "When you were a cop it might have been a raid, but I think what you are planning qualifies as a home invasion. We aren't cops."

He had a point. But I had one too. "I don't think these dirtbags will want to call the cops on us. This isn't an invasion... I'm calling it an... uh... intervention. Yeah, intervention. That is somewhat of socially conscious."

Tiki frowned, "Since when do you care about having a social conscious?"

"I don't. It just sounds better than home invasion." I insisted.

She nodded in agreement, which is rare.

Vance looked around. "Where is Monica?" She asked it in a weird way. I wasn't sure what her angle was.

"I think she booked out for higher ground. She didn't have the stomach for more violence. I can't say I blame her, Joan. She's been through a lot."

"Good. It's better she's gone."

Vance's expression was blank. It was her detective face. It didn't reveal acknowledgement, disagreement, or approval. It just was. When I see that face, I suspect she is not particularly happy about something. But I never guess what it is, and I don't like thinking about it. It makes my head hurt trying to guess a woman's thoughts.

Durd interrupted our non-conversation. "Let's take two cars."

We checked our weapons and ammunition, straightened ourselves out, and headed to see Guo... who I was sure would be happy to see us. I can't imagine there will be a problem.

Half an hour later, there was a problem. When you talk about twenty guys, you don't really expect twenty guys... you expect five guys and just assume that everyone was exaggerating when they said twenty guys... it's like a figure of speech. Twenty guys... same thing as 'particularly nice weather,' or 'tickle your ass with a feather...' just something people say. But in *this* case, there are at *least* twenty guys... none of them appeared to be slouches.

I got on our comms, "Everybody drive around the other block. We come in from two sides. We'll approach from the south."

We reset, slip like we were a flight of jet fighters and made another pass. I stomped on the gas as I cleared the last corner of our approach, bouncing up onto the sidewalk quite briskly I might say, and plowed into four unsuspecting guys who were just sitting there doing bad guy stuff. They went flying. Unfortunately, none of them were badly hurt. Seconds later, we are all outside in the condo landscaping, fighting like we were in a professional wrestling Battle Royal. But it was a fight in finely cared-for jungle foliage and sculpted weaving concrete walks and curbs, rather than a squared circle of canvas and ropes.

About half the bad guys ran inside the building to protect the man currently in command, Mister Guo.

Of the group that stayed to fight, I had two of them beating on me like I was a snare drum. Maybe Vance was on to something about that 'old guy' business. I clearly wasn't winning fast enough and although I was throwing plenty of good punches, I felt like I needed my house slippers and a nap. The long-ago-learned karate bullshit I knew kicked into automatic mode. I threw an inside middle block stopping an attack from the side and then I front kicked a guy in the solar plexus as he was trying to stab me. He sucked air. I triple punched his face, then threw an elbow strike against the temple of the other guy. Solar plexus guy collapsed in a heap sucking air. Temple strike guy went limp. I might have killed him. Awkward.

I saw Tiki was in trouble. I don't care how good you are at fighting, a small group of two-hundred-pound thugs usually win over a lone ninety pound woman every time. Even though she was getting overwhelmed, her technique remained perfect. She went into a low stance and punched a guy in the nuts, then did a spin, sweeping her leg behind another guy knocking him off his feet. A third guy bear-hug grabbed her from behind though and seemed to be squeezing the air out of her lungs.

I sprinted to her aid and from the rear, grabbed the guy's hands, twisting them back and inwards behind him, ripping tendons along the way. Tiki got her footing and mule kicked him in the testicles so hard it sounded like someone threw a tomato against a brick wall. She ducked down, locked an elbow around his knee, spinning him, while I kawhapped him in the snot locker with all the force I could pack behind my petite two-hundred-and-thirty-plus pound frame, delivering a left-handed front punch. She stood and twisted, and he went down quick, flopping on his back like a castrated penguin. I think we all know what that looks like. He cracked his head on the concrete pretty hard too upon landing. He was out.

I caught my partner out of the corner of my eye. Vance was all business. Of the ten or so guys we were fighting outside, she only had one and she was beating him senseless with a set of brass knuckles. Old school cop style.

Nicolo had three on him. He somehow blasted them in the face with some flaming magic shit, like throwing fire out of his hands. I hate magic. I never know what the hell is going on or why. But I had to admit, that fire trick was some bad ass shit. He followed up with palm heel strikes, elbows, and groin kicks.

Nicolo was a traffic cop in his younger years so fistfights were as normal to him as brushing his teeth or scratching his butt. He was fine.

Durd was zip tying the unconscious ones and dragging them into the courtyard area out of sight. This being Miami proper, no one called the cops on us.

One more guy jumped me, but before I could do anything Tiki cracked him on the skull with a big rock she found in the landscaping. I punched him in the lower belly. He collapsed in a heap of puke and blood.

It didn't take long to roll up this first batch of guys. I headed for the main door. Surprisingly it was unguarded. Maybe door security was one of our already vanquished goon's responsibility. We made way to Chen's condo in search of Mister Guo. We were hot, sweaty, pissed off, and all looked like we fell off a turnip truck onto a dusty road. I better add tired to that list too. This kicking ass thing is hard work. Especially if you are old enough to collect social security.

I noticed Nicolo and Dourdhoff were getting a little ripe. Neither had bathed since we launched this fiasco. I made them take the stairs. I didn't want their stinky asses in the elevator with the rest of us.

Two minutes later, Tiki, Vance, and I arrived at the door. I pulled my gun and kicked it in. The door went surprisingly easy. My foot didn't even hurt.

Guo was standing behind a wall of the ten remaining goons and said those famous words that I find quite discouraging.

"Get them!"

Unfortunately, they followed orders well and attempted to 'get' us.

I counter-yelled a semi-heroic command of my own. "Run!"

We turned and ran. We're professional investigators. We're not stupid.

Unfortunately again, the elevator doors were closed and the bad guys were almost on our asses in the hallway. "Follow me!" I zigged, then I zagged. The women did too. We got to the stairwell and I started taking four at a time on the steps. We made our way down a level when I decided we could make a stand in the narrow corridor of the stairwell.

I turned and ran back up the stairs. I only made it a foot when a goon executed an effective flying tackle on me and we hit the ground with a whoomp... and that 'whoomp' was me sucking for air.

The guy wasn't that big, so I stuck my foot up and into his crotch and then launched kicked him like a Judo Guru up and over the stairwell. I took a second to catch my breath.

I saw Tiki's underwear again as she ran over the top of me to engage the next two guys in line coming down.

Vance knocked out the new guy on top of me with a head shot from her brass knuckles. He went to sleepy town.

I got to my feet and the three of us started fighting for our lives. Durd and Nico soon appeared and joined the melee.

I punched faces until my arms felt like lead. I'd grab a guy and pull him down and around behind me so the guys could stomp on him while I picked out another.

We were bloodied but we made our way back up the stairs over a bloody pile of goons and went back to the condo.

Guo seemed shocked that we were still alive, he was alone, and we were back in his face.

He pulled a gun.

We all pulled guns.

He fired one round that went high and wild.

We fired forty-seven rounds between us that left him looking like a pile of shredded raw meat. But he was still twitching.

Damn it. Another lead who seemed to have gotten himself shot somehow. How does that keep happening?

I kneeled down and whispered a lie into his ear, or what was left of his ear, "My friend here is a doctor. We can save you... just tell me who is in charge of the casino scam."

He began to whisper back, "Go f..."

He never finished the sentence. One final twitch and he was dead as they come. I suppose he was trying to say, 'Go find the Lord,' which is always good advice.

In the spirit of good will, I said a few words over his mortal remains. "Guo, you were somewhat tough looking, and perhaps kind of mean in your own way, but definitely not bulletproof. See you in hell, punk."

I'm not usually so sentimental but my brain is rattled from all this fisticuffs and blasting, and I'm in need of a drink.

I started giving directions to my obviously dismayed staff. "Find a pillowcase. Gather their weapons, shell casings, and any of our debris. Durd, dump the weapons in a swamp somewhere. Everybody else search the joint for phones, notebooks, safes, money, contraband, and computers.

Tiki found a kilo of cocaine in a safe she said was left open. I suspect she opened it as that was within her skillset.

"Give it to me. Everyone wrap up and get to the cars."

I covered my face with my handkerchief and broke the kilo. I covered everything I could in the room with fine white powder, leaving myself an exit route so I didn't make cocaine footprints for a forensic guy to find and match to my size eleven-wide oxfords.

The Miami Police would blame this scene on being a Monday. Their interest would be minimal as a pile of dead thugs dusted in coke is about as compelling as an overdue parking meter in this town. The remaining hoods, who we just beat the shit out of, would see their boss was dead and disappear into the streets of Miami like the cockroaches they were before the cops arrived.

I was tired and pissed off and without a legitimate lead. It was time to go back to the safe house and figure out next steps.

An hour and a bottle of Jim Beam later, our merry band was not at one with the universe. We were out of leads and everyone who had answers for us was dead. In the detective game, we call that something that rhymes with trucked.

"Becker," Vance said. "We might have met our goal. Monica is safe, so safe we don't even know where she is, the killers are dead, and we are out of people to shoot."

Nicolo disagreed, "We don't know who ordered it. That is the job. That is who has to pay."

Nicolo wasn't wrong. I added, "Remember, Conti is a client too. He wants to know who is trying to take down their casino... and the tech... apparently, that has some significant value. We can't quit yet."

Durd nodded vigorously, "The ability to launder digital funds they have developed is light years ahead of what is going on in crypto now. If that curly-headed creep in the Bahamas with the Olive Oil girlfriend had this tech when they did the big bitcoin scam, they wouldn't be looking at a hundred indictments and lawsuits today."

We agreed. This thing was far from over on a bunch of different levels. Someone was making a move and as long as they were out there, none of us were safe... except maybe Monica who hopefully is chilling out under another name on a beach in a non-extradition country. She might be the only smart one in this mess.

I made a decision. "I need to call Conti... he deserves a progress report... and maybe he's found out something on his end."

Vance agreed. "That's as good a plan as any... I'm ordering pizzas."

"That's an even better plan. Get a case of beer too. But call it in under a fake name and have Worm pick them up. We need to maintain operational security for a while yet, at least."

Vance picked up her phone and started dialing for pizza. "You got it, Becker."

I walked out to the balcony to make a call. I dialed the private number Conti gave me.

A voice came on, "Conti."

"It's Becker."

"I heard there was a decline in Miami's hood population, Becker.

"People hear all kinds of stuff... but I don't think it's safe yet, so stay under protection until I call you again."

"Yeah, I have no desire to go anywhere until this is settled."

I was getting the impression Conti wasn't as

tough as he acted.

"Good... and call me if you hear anything."

"I will... so far, the board is solidifying... as long as we're alive, nobody is taking over this casino or its technology."

"That's good news, Conti... I'll be in touch."

It wasn't really good news. It was another dead end. But I like to remain optimistic in front of clients. I started thinking about pizza and a cold Butt Whisker beer, my favorite brand. Beer and pizza solves a lot of problems.

An hour later I was stretched out on one of the beds working on my third slice and fourth brewsky. I started thinking about my little bedroom romp with Monica. That was even more fun than fist fighting all of Chen's thugs. Where could she be now? It's best I don't know... but I'd kind of *like* to know.

Tiki banged on the door and brought me another beer. "Boss, you need beer. You do better wish some beer. Makes you smarter."

I chose not to argue. When she's right, she's right. "Thanks, Tiki... have a seat."

She parked it in the big recliner in the corner of the room. "What's up?"

"Who do you think is behind this? I'll be real honest with you. I'm at a loss."

"I don't know, boss, and I don't care. I'm just here to kick ass."

Good old Tiki... her badassery reminded me of my detectives on the police department. None of them could believe someone would pay us to beat the crap out of criminals. I don't think it's like that anymore though.

I changed the direction of our conversation. "What do you think of Monica?"

"She skank."

That startled me. "What?"

"I sense she skank... I don't like her, boss..."

"Why?"

"She seduce you. Why would any honest woman do that?"

"No, she didn't."

"Yes, she did. You bang-bang."

"Absolutely not."

"Stop lie."

"You're fired."

"I quit."

"Never mind, you can stay.

"Fine."

She got up and left. I think she still works here. With her, it's difficult to know some days.

So now it was just me in the room, a man who apparently has no appeal to honest women, drinking a beer and eating a slice of supreme pizza while trying to solve an unsolvable problem. And everyone who can help me find the answer is dead.

It might be time to call in the cops. Although I'd prefer to not have my name attached to a case that already has a bunch of dead criminals involved.

Or, I could return to the scene of the crime. That works on television. And when did television ever lie to us... well, other than all the time... never. But now that I think about it, it's usually the killer who they say returns to the scene of the crime... but that works too.

I put down the beer, went to the bathroom, cleaned myself up a little, then went out into the main room to dispense some orders and directions with my newfound clarity.

My crew was still gathered around the big dining room table, so I got to the point. "Listen up. I'm going back to the casino. This case is colder than a mother-in-law's kiss. I'm going back to the beginning and starting over at the casino. You guys disperse back to hotels and lay low until you hear from me."

Vance wasn't buying it. "You don't go alone, Becker. We just went over this. You're old, fat, and possibly drunk. I'll go."

"No."

"No?"

"No... you can't go. I need you to protect Nicolo. Tiki can come." I was a little pissed off about her wise crack, even though it was accurate, except for the drunk part.

"Fair enough... Tiki can watch your back... It's just that...we just can't lose you, Becker...."

She appeared confused about what she just said.

Like she didn't mean it that way. Then she blurbed out the rest.

"… You sign our paychecks."

I was touched.

Tiki grabbed my arm, "Let's go, I'm tired of hanging out here. You old and might die before we get there."

I growled over my shoulder at the team. "We'll be at the casino if you need us… and don't let Nicolo get killed and don't let him shoot anyone else's business off."

I heard Nicolo mumbling something about not needing protection, but I ignored it. Tiki and I walked out to the Jaguar and headed to the scene of the crime.

We rode silently for five minutes before I put my cards on the table. "You know we're not going to the casino, Tiki…"

"I know, boss… that's why you leave Vance behind. But it's *fine* if Tiki goes to prison. You a shitty boss."

"Do you want out?"

"No, I go… Might be fun."

The commission of a burglary is often frowned up by those who license private investigators for reasons only they seem to understand. I know, in the scheme of things, we've done much worse than a little professional B&E, but those little misunderstandings have all been cleaned up and forgotten. Getting caught by a patrol car while one is in a residence other than your own, without permission, and at night, can be awkward however, and might result in a lengthy jail term... So, our rule is... don't get caught.

If Tiki and I get busted and disavowed by the licensing bureau, then Vance, who is legitimately in the dark on our activities, can take over and still run the business until we get forgiven or do our time.

Luca's residence is really the place where this all started in my opinion. That's where I met Monica. That's where Luca was last seen acting all carefree and alive before the parking lot snatch and grab that led to his unfortunate crispy critter situation.

The question of the day is, what was Monica looking for, and did she find it? I don't think she told us everything. But nobody really ever tells 'everything,' so that didn't really worry me. We were missing something important in this case. We needed to find whatever that was.

Monica mentioned she was snooping around Luca's house for cash and a burner phone. What if there was more? And what about the mysterious cache of money? He was a talker... He was an operator who liked to play gangster. He might have been careless in other ways.

We needed to toss the joint. Tiki's life experience as a prostitute and sex-trafficking victim would help. She knows how to find where people hide things. I knew her history. She did in-call work for a while. That's where she would go to the customers house to give a 'massage' or to provide 'dance entertainment.' But instead of happy time, the pimp would have her drug the john and then search the place for hidden stashes of cash, dope, or valuables. She was like a combination of hound dog and pawn shop manager. She knew where things might be and what they were worth. We'd need that skillset here tonight.

We parked around the corner and hopped a fence. We stealthed our way across the yard to the back door.

In the shadows, I squatted down by the door lock. "I can pick this lock. Hold a light for me, Tiki." I reached in my back pocket for my picks.

"How about first I try to twist the knob, Becker."

"Nobody leaves their door unlocked anymore, Tiki. But knock yourself out." I was a little disappointed in her amateur approach to this problem.

She twisted the knob.

The door swung open.

Chagrin is a word I rarely use. But I know what it means. I was soaking in it at the moment.

She gave me a dirty grin. "Knock your own self out, Becker."

I stared at her for a long moment.

She looked back at me for a longer one.

Then she added, "You a dick! Tiki is champion."

I have nothing.

A moment later and we were inside Luca's house.

"Tiki, you check the back, I'll hit his office."

She gave me a quick nod and disappeared into the darkness.

I took the office because that would be the easiest. I'm not ashamed to say Tiki is better at this than I am.

I went through the desk. I found a small notebook and some thumb drives. I took them. I couldn't find a safe. I checked the wastebasket for discarded notes.

Nothing.

I checked the bookcases.

There was a gun behind a row of classic books that had never been opened. It was a 1903 Colt automatic pistol. The pocket hammerless model. He wouldn't need it anymore. I secured the weapon and stuffed it in my jacket pocket. The magazine was loaded but the chamber wasn't charged. Remember what Mister Worm always says, it's legal to steal off a dead guy. So, technically, I didn't commit much of a crime.

I looked under carpets and chair cushions. I checked behind the art and photos on the wall. I noticed something. No photos of Monica... he had a few photos of another woman though, along with a photo of our former governor, the ex-president's brother. He had quite a few photos with political figures and celebrities. I always figure when there is a photo taken of two people smiling at the camera in a public setting and at least one of them is famous, they probably don't really know each other over ninety-five percent of the time.

Who was the other woman? Maybe Monica was just side entertainment rather than the main squeeze. Was she exaggerating her relationship with Luca?

I decided to take one of the pictures of Luca for the file. I picked one of Luca and that hot female singer, I can't remember her name, but she was looking especially hot in this photograph... it was totally evidence. I took it out of the frame. Behind the picture, however, I noticed an address and a series of numbers. The numbers looked like a lock combination... was that the storage locker full of money? I didn't think that part was really true. I just played along with Monica when she told me about it. My policy is never tell someone they are full of shit until you know they are full of shit. Every mob related fairy tale has a storage locker full of money component. Ask that goofy news guy... I can't remember his name... he had a mustache. doesn't matter. Nobody keeps money that way except big time drug traffickers. This might be something else though. I checked a couple of other pictures, but they didn't have a code and an address behind them. This might be something.

"Becker!"

I heard Tiki's loud whisper and turned. She was standing in the doorway with a briefcase and a pillowcase. It looked like she scored.

"Yeah."

"We got to go. Nothing else here." she insisted. "We stay too long now."

The lady is correct. "Fine. Let's get out of here."

We took our booty and left the way we came in. We were in the backyard clambering over the fence when I heard a car pull up out front and stop. It was either security or someone else had the same idea we did.

"Who is that?" she whispered, this time softly.

"No time to check who it is. We got to get out of here, Tiki."

Tiki's formal diction went out the window. She was in action mode again. "You go, Becker. You old and fat. I hide… I see what up. Pick me up outside fence in hour."

Does anyone follow orders anymore?

But she wasn't wrong. It would be good to find out who our new searchers were and what they were looking for. Tiki is tiny and can hide… I'm not that old or fat, but I am big and difficult to conceal. I hopped over the wall, fell on my butt, gut up, and limped my way to the car, and waited.

I fished around the glovebox for a bottle of generic pain relief pills I picked up at the grocery store. I was a little sore from the fall. Anybody would be regardless of age. Age doesn't have anything to do with it. I found a bottled water in the back seat and swallowed four of them.

An hour later I picked Tiki up when I saw her slither over the wall like an iguana. She slid into the passenger seat, and we got out of there.

"What did you find?"

"New bad guys."

"What?"

"Somebody we don't know. They went right to bedroom and got something out of bed headboard. Some microphone or camera or something. They were cleaning up for someone. Spies maybe."

"Spies?"

"Well, guys who make evidence go away."

"Oh, yeah... but what evidence?"

"I don't know but one of them say they have three more places to clean tonight."

"What does that mean?"

"It means they go three more places and get more camera."

"No, I mean, why are they doing this and who are they doing it for?"

"Then just say that. You talk in circle, Becker. Nobody with good English ever understand you sometimes."

"Shut up, Tiki... I'm thinking."

"Okay, boss."

She sat back quietly. I was surprised she wasn't mad that I told her to put a sock in it. She finally did something I asked her to do without arguing. I'd have to mark this in my calendar. I've found that it is either extremely easy or extremely difficult to offend Tiki... She is a mysterious and unpredictable woman, but she does her job and does it well, interpersonal communications barriers aside.

"I imagine that those guys were the extortion crew cleaning up loose ends. They might hit all of the board's houses or wherever they have illicit affairs. That would explain a lot, right?"

"Tiki is the shut up."

I should have known it wasn't over.

"Fine. I'm just thinking out loud."

"Then that is not thinking. That is saying. For a boss, you not a good communicator, Becker."

I was almost pissed off but realized she was technically correct. It was my turn to be the shut up.

Tiki started talking to me again. I guess she decided we were even now. "Becker, you said she has location of storage full of cash."

"I don't remember telling anyone that, but that's true. How did you know?"

"I overheard you talking to Joe Campbell on the phone."

Joe Campbell was a Deputy Director at the Florida Department of Law Enforcement. I did give him a heads up that I had a lead on a stash of illicit funds and might need a quick response when the case broke. Joe was a Highway Patrol officer when

I was a beat cop. We'd been sharing coffee and lies for over thirty years… or maybe forty years… where does the time go? But I trust him and he seems to trust me. He saved our asses in the last big investigation we did with the dead British spy and the Columbians. I had no idea Tiki overheard that call. She's a good detective. How can I get mad at her for eavesdropping? It's what we do.

"So, what's your point?" I asked.

"When someone is on the run, they grab the money… period."

I noticed her diction had improved to the point I could barely notice her accent. I wonder if she does that on purpose? But she had a point. I gave her the photo.

"Tiki, look at the back of this and figure out where it is."

She used her phone to illuminate the back of the photo, then used it to check something on her map application. "This is funny." She giggled, which is uncharacteristic but was kind of cute.

"What?"

"That hot lady in the picture is Scarlett… the storage locker is called Scarlett Storage. He made a clue."

"Hmmm… interesting. Give me directions."

We crossed town and found the place. There was an on-duty guard at the gate when I pulled into the entrance. Tiki leaned over me displaying significant cleavage to the security man while using her helpless female voice.

"Mister Guard. I left my wallet and keys in locker this morning. This nice neighbor man give me a ride here to get back."

I gave him an eyebrow wiggle to suggest that helping this poor girl might bear some reward.

The middle-aged, heavy-set man in the wrinkled gray uniform looked confused. But he was listening... and looking. Tiki's boobs revived his sense of chivalry.

She pushed the issue. "I leave my purse with you. Keep honest."

Where did she get that purse? Oh, she probably lifted it from the house.

The slovenly security man smiled and winked at me knowingly... "Sure, I suppose I can let you in, if your friend doesn't mind waiting."

Being agreeable was the right move. "I don't mind."

The guard let Tiki pass. I waited outside and made small talk with him, sharing lurid but fictitious tales of my flirty and sexy neighbor lady, which he lapped up like a cat slurping tuna juice. This led me to believe that working security at a storage locker facility is a very lonely job.

She wasn't gone long, but it seemed like a long time. I ran out of torrid stories quickly. I was trying to remember the plot to the Skin-a-Max classic Fiona Does Philadelphia, when she came walking back to the guard shack, strutting her stuff like a runway model.

The guard liked that action more than my story and seemingly forgot all about my poorly told tall tales of eroticism.

Tiki got in the car and we drove away, but not before she gave the guard a kiss on the face cheek and a squeeze of his butt cheek. I think she made his day. He'll probably never quit this job, just in the off chance she might come back someday.

When we were a block from the storage facility, I asked the big question. "Did you find the money?"

"No… locker was empty. But someone had been there. I went in office and checked the log."

"That fast?"

"Tiki no mess around, Becker. You know that."

"What did you find?"

"That was Luca's locker. He was there morning of day he went missing. Someone else was there today… used dead man's name."

"So, if the cash existed, he moved it."

"Yeah, that's what I think."

"Good work, Tiki ChaCha… you're a pretty darned good detective."

"Yeah, boss. I know that. I keep telling you that. Glad you remember."

She is a difficult person to compliment. So I quit trying.

"Let's go meet the others. See if they came up with anything."

"Sounds good," she said as she sorted through

her pillowcase full of pilfered items.

You know, in the scheme of things, some cases go easier than others. Other cases seem to wind up with a bunch of dead guys, zero leads, and lost money... I think we are working the latter.

CHAPTER 9 - THE HURRIER YOU GO, THE BEHINDER YOU GET

Everyone was getting antsy. The case was dragging out and it seemed like we were getting further behind by the hour. Another morning was rolling up on us. Another sleepless night. Even with Chen and Guo out of the picture, at this point in the case, we might still be at risk. We don't have the name of the shot-caller... the boss. And now there was this new crew picking up surveillance gear. Obviously very professional. That kind of talent is welcome on either side of the law.

I said what I had to say. "I'm thinking about calling in the cops on this."

That statement earned me an unusually loud set of groans and some dramatic eye rolls from the team.

"Seriously. We are out of leads. The money is missing. One of our clients skipped town. There are some uncomfortable-to-explain dead guy situations we need to *avoid* talking to the police about... and the casino is still in some significant peril. We just don't know from whom. It could be mob guys, cartel, guys, inside guys, outside guys... maybe Chinese guys... we just don't know. And I am not sure where to turn next. I'm out of ideas."

Vance cleared her throat like she had something to say.

"What's on your mind, Joan. Spit it out."

"I'm not ready to quit. When we were cops, what did we do when a case goes dry?"

I thought about it before answering. "We shake the shit out of it until something happens."

"Yeah."

"But what do we shake the shit out of?"

"Conti."

"He's a client."

"Yeah, but he's a good place to start shaking. Let's get him out of the casino and have a heart to heart. We won't get traction with him on his own turf. And hey, the worst he can do is fire us."

She had a point.

"Well, I might be able to talk him out. But I want Campbell at FDLE dialed up on everyone's phone in case this turns to shit on us. I'll let him know we are working something hot involving the casino... he'll be interested."

Durd commented. "Makes sense... we just leave out the parts regarding the late Chen and Guo, right?"

I answered, "Never heard of them."

The others all shrugged and made the '*I have no idea what you are talking about*' face. Durd, being a genius with an IQ that Einstein would envy, caught on quickly. "Yeah, I never heard of them either, Becker."

"Good. Here's what we're going to do."

For once, everybody was immediately on board with my plan.

I made the call and Conti picked up on the first ring.

"Conti."

"Becker here. Can you talk?"

"Sure."

"We need to meet."

"Come on up."

"No, I want to meet on my boat. I'll dock it behind the Venetia on 15th. We'll be safe. Just use the parking garage and walk out to the docks."

"Why?"

"We're about to wrap this up. I don't want anyone else at the casino to know what's up until you've had time to digest it.

"No offense, Becker, but why should I trust you? I'm taking a big chance leaving here."

"The physical threats to your safety have been dealt with. You're my client. If I screw you over, I'm done in Miami forever. You'll be safe."

He was quiet for longer than I liked. Then he got agreeable.

"Fine. When?"

"Sunset."

Another long pause... he seemed more indecisive than he was the last time I talked to him.

"See you then."

I disconnected and

"It's on. Vance, you're with me on the boat."

She nodded. "I have a change of clothes here. Let me switch out and I'll meet you at the car."

Vance and I retrieved my thirty-seven-foot Edgewater center console from the dock behind my condo in Lauderdale-by-the-Sea and made way for the docks in Miami. It was good to get out on the water. A couple of hours of breathing salt air was what I needed. The rest of the team would drive down and be staged in positions around the meeting. Nicolo was assigned to be set up in the parking garage. His job was to let us know when Conti arrived and if he came alone. Tiki and Worm were to take positions around the docks to intercept any unexpected interference. Durd, as usual, would coordinate operations from his van, hopefully with a drone and our monitoring equipment in full play.

The plan was in place. The time was soon. The outcome of what this Hail Mary effort would bring was as of yet, unknown.

We weren't in a rush. I could have made the twenty-eight-mile run on the outside, taking a quit turn out to the ocean, getting there in less than an hour, but I decided to cruise along down the intra-coastal. We had the time. I needed the break. I needed time to think.

I noticed, not that I could help but notice, Vance switched into very short cotton shorts, canvas boat shoes, and a deep cut silk blouse that if nothing else, allowed her to tan her cleavage without obstruction, not that I noticed her cleavage. Working with beautiful women every day takes its toll on a man. Even at my age. I constantly am in a state of 'forced ignoring' of the obvious.

Apparently, Joan, who wasn't a real mariner like me, thought this was a good time to talk. I hate talk. Time at sea isn't for talk. It's for being quiet. Everybody knows that.

"Becker," she began with what seemed like an unnecessary amount of caution in her voice, "Have you ever thought of retirement?"

She took off her RayBans when she said that. She must be serious.

I stayed ambiguous on the topic. "Right now I'm thinking about it, you know, maybe in a few years... why?"

"Look, I've never made as much money in my life as I've made working for you. We, us...the business... we have crazy good cash flow. You were already rich... and... to be honest, you aren't getting any younger. Why don't you just enjoy your life. I can run this business for you and pump a fat check into your account every month. Maybe you should retire, Becker. Spend every day out on the boat."

"What makes you think I don't enjoy this?"

"Well, you get beat up and shot sometimes. That's not fun. And to be honest... again..." She made an extraordinarily long pause before continuing. She looked off toward shore then looked me in the eye. "I don't want anything to happen to you."

I suddenly felt weird. Where was this going?

"What? What would happen to me? I can't be killed by conventional means... I think you underestimate me, Joan. I'm in my prime."

I thought that would make her laugh. It didn't. She was as serious as a Mormon in a brewery.

She clarified her statement, leaving me even more rattled. "I mean, I care about you, Becker."

This time she eye-locked me... I blinked. She didn't.

I enunciated my next words extremely slowly for reasons I do not know. "Care... about... me?" This is creepy, nobody cares about me. I don't even care about me. Well, Mister Worm cares about me because I pay him to care about me. That's the definition of a butler.

She didn't break eye contact. My mind was flying. I pulled back on the throttle and let the boat drift to a stop.

Have you ever had a time when you are so confused you think you might have slipped into one of those parallel universe deals you hear about on YouTube? When you wonder if the person in front of you is talking to you or someone else standing behind you? I was feeling that. I also felt her left hand slip gently along the crook of my neck. Not in a choke out way, but in an affectionate way. I'm not used to affection.

"Becker, we've been together a while... and I never said anything. But I need to be honest. I might have feelings for you."

"Vance? What? Me? Joan, I'm old and disgusting. You're young and beautiful."

"Becker, you are in your... whatevers, and I'm in my forties now. We're not that far off. You aren't disgusting. You're far from over-the-hill. I just don't want anything happening that might... end this."

She slid into my arms, and we kissed.

I didn't see that coming.

I didn't mind it either.

I'd admired everything about Joan. I like her. She is gorgeous. She gets cop culture, hell she was a cop. She's tough. She is smart... but what could she possibly see in me?

Joan whispered in my ear. "Becker, you are the only one who doesn't see the man the rest of us see in you. You're the one, Becker. You're the one for me."

I had been denying my normal male attraction to her for so long, it was difficult to change gears. but not impossible.

This time, I kissed her. It didn't feel weird, it felt

right. Maybe I'm not done... Maybe I'm not over-the-hill. Joan was amazing and we get along... sometimes it's like we are really close. We think alike. We have the same interests. She's reliable. Should I let this happen? Or should I protect her from me. I'm not an easy person to be around.

I stumbled through my next words. "Joan, we need to talk more... after the case. We can take the boat to the Bahamas, chill out a few days in the sand, and sort it out. No rush. But I want to be sure. Will that work?

She smiled and gave me a peck on the cheek. "Yeah, Becker. That works."

She leaned into me as I piloted us south to Miami. I put my arm around her waist as normally as if I'd done it a hundred times. If we both lived through the next twelve hours, this thing might work out. My Irish side told me not to think about it. I would jink it. So, I just took in the sun and the smells and the feel of cruising the intra-coastal with a beautiful woman on my arm snuggled up against me.

Life takes some weird turns.

Not all of those turns are bad.

It was close to sunset when we arrived. I called ahead to the marina and reserved a transient slip. The short-notice reservation wasn't a problem. I'd been there many times for lunch at Mike's place on the 9th floor, so they knew me.

I steered us into a side-tie. Joan hopped off and secured the bow. I gave the helm a turn and guided the back of the boat in, killed the engine, and then hopped off and tied up the stern. When the boat was secured, we turned on the ear comms Durd set up for us. Durd's comm units provided a much better system than anything we ever had on the police department, but that's Durd... the best at what he does. Nerd stuff.

"Everyone in position?" I asked on the general communications channel.

I heard the team each respond with 'check.'

"Then it's a waiting game. Get ready."

We didn't wait long.

Nicolo came on the air. "Conti just rolled in driving his gray Bentley."

I asked a stupid question I already knew the answer to, just because as the boss, I felt compelled to ask a question... the reason I miss working alone number three-ninety-five. "Can you follow him without getting spotted?"

"I have another disguise. He won't see me. Guaranteed."

"Copy that."

Mister Worm came on the line, "Copy don't shoot the person in disguise."

That statement made my head hurt on many, many levels.

Nicolo was back on. "He's coming in on foot heading for the sidewalk on 15th."

"Copy."

"He has a couple of guys."

"What guys?"

"One of them is head of security for the casino... the other is a big guy... maybe six-foot-seven. Ugly."

Worm came online again. "Copy six-seven and ugly. I'll take him, Becker."

I barked, "Listen up, we aren't '*taking*' anybody unless things go south, we're just putting the squeeze on our primary."

Worm came back on, "Copy squeeze my primary."

I heard Vance snickering.

He's doing this on purpose.

I got back on the horn. "We see him. But he's alone now, approaching the boat down the embarcadero... he's on the docks... we'll be off the air. You can monitor... we won't hear you."

Some people enter, others make an entrance. Conti was dressed in what had to be a bespoke two-thousand-dollar light blue linen suit. He sported legit alligator loafers, a silk t-shirt that looked like he just stepped out of a Miami Vice episode. One wrist had a solid gold Audemars Piguet Royal Oak wristwatch and the other had a ten millimeter thick fourteen karat gold chain. He wore a pair of folding Persol sunglasses. His hair, which he had a lot of, was perfectly coifed and oiled to make him look just like a movie star. The dark tan and perfect teeth finished the look.

Power looks are intimidating to most people. You can dress a turd up like Conti and people will show instant respect for it. Well, maybe not a turd, but... I admit, he was intimidating, even for me.

The two security guys waited just inside the metal gate at the dock staring at us like a pair of tag team wrestlers reading to reclaim their belt.

"Permission to come aboard, Captain?" Conti requested.

"Granted."

Conti stepped over and onto the boat from the dock. "Becker... who is your lovely... uh... friend?" He gave Vance a seductive once over, eyeing her like a piece of tasty steak he was ready to stick a fork into.

So is everyone in the casino business a horn dog?"

I kept it professional, even though I wanted to kick his ass. "This is my business partner, Joan Vance. Joan, meet Mister Conti."

"Please, Gino. I insist." He said as if he was granting her the privilege of using his first name in trade for sexual favors.

Is my imagination running away with me? Am I jealous? Probably not, I'm very reasonable.

He laid on a bunch of charm, perhaps an overwhelming pile of charm. I might be close to losing my girl before she is officially my girl.

She seemed smitten with the handsome casino owner... a guy who hangs out with celebrities and has a ton of money... I don't know what she sees in him. He smells funny and I think he has lifts in his shoes. And the poor alligators who were murdered to make those shoes... how can you forget about them?

"My pleasure, Gino," she said in a voice silky as his shirt as she reached out to shake his hand.

He bowed, took it in his, and kissed the hand gently...for an excessively long time. Gross. I wonder if I would get kicked out of the marina for throwing him overboard. Nobody likes a woman seducer. I'm sure there won't be repercussions. Next, he will probably try to lick her face... then I shoot him.

Joan looked over her shoulder at me and gave me the 'grow up' look, then winked impishly. We were good. She's acting, I'm an idiot. But I was glad I got the reality check. I'm back in control.

I noticed the air suddenly cooled like it does over the water when sunset is imminent. A big fish jumped out of the water about ten yards off the bow. The splash seemed unusually clear and sharp.

I was getting in the zone... focused... ready. Conti is just a pretty boy who smells really good, I'm the bad ass here. I need to get my pecking order straight and deal with this clown.

I got Conti's attention refocused to me as we all sat down on the deck chairs under the shade provided by an adjacent sailboat.

"Why are we here, Becker," he asked a bit impatiently, like me saving his casino was an imposition on his time.

"We're here to get to the bottom of the death of Luca and the death of Sonechka. When those cases are closed, we will know the name of the party who is trying to take over your casino."

He looked a bit more concerned than I expected him to be. "So, you have an idea who the murderer is?"

"I think so."

I was lying, I had no idea. But I wanted to see his reaction.

"So, who is it?" he asked, a bit impatiently.

"Before I tell you," I stalled, "Tell me more about your relationship with Luca."

I was fishing for information, I hoped he didn't pick up on that.

"Luca?"

"Yeah... the first dead guy in this thing. The board member who wound up as alligator snacks."

My words made him visibly nervous. So nervous, he started looking around like he was hunting an escape route.

Interesting.

Then he puffed up. He was too pretty to get tough. I had him and he knew it. It pissed him off. He tried to bluster. "I don't like the direction this is going, Becker. Remember, pal, you work for me."

"Yeah, I do." I left that there without inflection. He didn't know if I was agreeing or being sarcastic, just like I wanted. He was off balance and confused… and maybe a little afraid.

I gave him some more. "Somebody has a stockpile of cash. Possibly embezzled from the casino. That somebody has partners. Someone on the inside who can control things, direct things, hide things."

I saw a bead of sweat break out on his brow. I think Vance saw it too. She took a shot at rattling his cage even more… the old good cop, bad cop routine.

"Look Conti," she said softly, "If that person needs a way out, there is a way out. But they would have to trust us with the truth… the whole truth. I know you understand what I'm saying."

I'm not so sure he did understand. He looked like he might be filling the back of his pants.

Conti was done. His well tanned and groomed face appeared terribly sad. Clothes might make the man, but underneath the clothes there still has to be a man. He was learning that the hard way.

But then he tried defiance. One last kick at the devil before condemnation.

He yanked his phone out of his pocket and hit a button. A guy who looked like King Kong's ugly brother and Doyle Gilheaney, the head of casino security, came marching down the dock like storm troopers in a parade. Not just marching, quick marching... uh, Jogging. Now they are hauling ass. This is not good.

I saw Vance start to reach for her Glock back-up. She left her auto-mag below deck. I gave her a facial expression that said just wait.

In the brief piece of quiet we had before they made their move, I listened carefully to make sure no one could hear Durd's drone overhead capturing all of this on film.

I think Conti was as surprised as I was when Gilheaney and the Neanderthal approached the boat with guns in their hands.

"Doyle, there is no need for firearms. Just get me out of here." He turned his attention to me. "Becker, you're fired... and unfortunately, so is your beautiful colleague. I'll see you both in court for slander. Neither of you will ever work in this town again!"

Conti started to step on the gunwale and up to the dock when the cave man stuck a palm the size of a sheet of plywood out and pushed him back into the boat and onto his ass.

Gilheaney laughed. "Not so fast, Conti. Maybe you're the one who is fired."

Conti got to his feet in a felony huff... full of piss and vinegar, but not anxious to go to Fist City over it with these two.

"What the hell is this?" he demanded.

I watched for any opening as the two security men stepped down into the boat with guns held discreetly close to their bodies. There would be no gun grab today. No likelihood of success for a quick draw either.

Professionals.

Shit.

GIlheaney started giving orders. "Nyx, get their weapons. Everybody cooperate and you won't get shot."

The giant, who I guess is named Nyx, which is kind of scary, took our guns. It wasn't like fighting him for them would be a good idea. My gun was a forty-five and I wasn't sure it would drop the big bastard anyway. I wish Vance had her Auto-Mag.

"Okay, beautiful, untie the boat. Becker, take us out."

Well, I didn't see that coming either. Shit... and this day was going so well, too.

I noticed a little old lady moving quickly up the dock with a Glock in her paw. I whispered in my comm, "Not now," as I started the engine. No one else on the boat heard me.

Nicolo stood down. I had to admit, except for the hairy legs, that was a pretty good disguise.

Joan did as she was told. I fired up the motors and we headed out of the marina.

I asked the obvious. "Where too?"

"Out to sea, Becker... about fifteen miles should do."

I hoped the crew was picking all of this up. Because if our comms weren't transmitting, we were going to be the special guests of honor for a funeral at sea.

Luckily, everyone stayed top side. My M4 Benelli semi-automatic tactical shotgun and Joans AutoMag handgun were under the chart table cushions. If one of us could get down there, we might have a chance. In the meantime, it was a great opportunity to solve the case, even though I'd just been fired.

As I headed us out of the intra-coastal and into the Atlantic, I asked a question, "So it was you all along, Gilheaney?"

Unlike Bond villains, he didn't feel compelled to tell me the plan. "Just steer the boat, Becker." He handed me a slip of paper. Go to these coordinates. I read them and entered the numbers into my chart plotter. I turned east and followed the course.

I tried again, "So who else is in on it, obviously not Conti."

Gilheaney laughed, "Conti is a fool. They are all fools. The whole board. They knew what they had but they didn't use it. I could have made millions with that tech… for a while I did until Luca figured it out. But you don't have to worry about it."

Good, he was talking and was finding some joy in humiliating Conti. That was good and bad. It was good he was talking, but it was also bad in that it meant he was going to kill all of us. I wondered if the drone had a fifteen-mile range. I wondered if I was going to die before I kissed Vance again, which yesterday would have been a creepy thought to have. But things change. For the first time in a while, living seemed like something important. I tried to keep him talking.

"Look, you can't take over the board. When Conti turns up missing, the cops will be all over it."

Conti started to cry a little. He whimpered as he squatted down in the corner of the cockpit, "Why would I turn up missing?"

Gilheaney laughed. "I guess he isn't seeing the big picture."

I looked over my shoulder, back at Conti. "He's going to kill you, dumbass," I explained very politely.

"What?"

Gilheaney laughed loudly this time. I must have tickled his funny bone.

"No, no, no... I'm not going to kill you, Conti. The corrupt private eye you hired is going to kill you. He was behind the whole thing. You'll be remembered as a hero. The guy who tried to face down the extortionist. I might even erect a statue of you in the lobby. And soon, the four board members I have dossiers on will support my nomination to the board and then to chairman in honor of my heroic efforts in solving this horrible conspiracy."

I noticed Nyx was getting seasick... he was a little green around the gills, like we say in the pirate business. A thirty-seven-foot boat is a nice sized boat, but the ocean seems terribly big once you are out in it and suddenly thirty-seven feet seems terribly small. The experience of bobbing in vast open water, moving horizontally and vertically and laterally at the same time, the never-ending wind... it messes some people up. The question was, would his negative reaction to life at sea give us the chance to make our move?

We were closing in on the coordinates... there wasn't a lot of time left. Then things got weird.

CHAPTER 10 - A HELL OF A DAY AT SEA

It was dark, we were miles away from any ambient light. The sea was getting a little rough... it felt like we might see some weather.

My assessment of the situation hadn't improved. We were screwed.

Gilheaney looked over my shoulder at the chart plotter. He stuck a gun in my ribs to make sure I heard what he said next. "We're here. Kill the engines."

I did as ordered.

I tried to keep them talking. Whatever was going to happen, would happen soon.

"Gilheaney, did you consider that when you show up at a marina in my boat without me, someone will notice." I felt like that was a pretty good argument.

Gilheaney just shook his head like he was talking to a little kid, "I'm not going back in your boat, genius. This boat will sink... it will sink here, and you as Captain will go down with the ship. I don't think they will ever find you. Funny, huh?"

I didn't think it was funny at all.

Now I'm pissed. Nobody is authorized to sink my boat, except Mother Nature or Poseidon, and

I don't have any plans in mind that would incur their wrath to do so. I obey all the laws of the sea and all the superstitions of sailors. This bag of crap is not sinking my boat.

Then I wondered, how does he plan on getting back?

Vance decided to make a move. "I got to pee. Let me go use the head. You can stand outside the door if you want."

Gilheaney was surprisingly sympathetic. His confidence was high. What did he know? What was his plan?

"Go ahead. Nyx, keep an eye on her." he gave me a smug look. "Don't worry, Becker. It won't be too much longer."

I realized Gilheaney wasn't much of a boater either. He might not be seasick, but he didn't notice the subtle signs of motion sickness Nyx was demonstrating. An experienced Captain will see it right away. Anyone getting ill on board can quickly become an emergency situation if not promptly addressed. It's always better to interdict early rather than wait until after things get out of control. He also didn't calculate how little elbow room there is below deck. Vance knew. I knew. This was our moment.

Nyx stepped down into the cabin behind Vance. I could see her in the small gap between Nyx's shoulders and the bulkhead. I knew then that she was going for it. I didn't move.

I heard her voice from below.

"We keep the toilet paper here. Let me grab a roll first. This is so embarrassing."

The sickly behemoth didn't really care what she did. He knew that the moment he stepped below deck he felt markedly worse. In the cabin, he couldn't look over the horizon to steady his equilibrium. It's the worst place to be if you don't feel good. He was sick... he was about to puke.

Vance made her move.

She snatched the forty-four AutoMag out from under the cushion, spun around, and mag-dumped his giant ass while his massive body was jammed in the hatch. He couldn't move, the quarters were too close.

The sound was deafening. The muzzle flash below deck looked like an explosion. A big glob of Nyx's brain flew back and hit Gilheaney in the face. He dropped his weapon.

It was my turn.

I swung as hard as I could and connected to the side of his head with a right cross. He stumbled over a chair and fell. I dove on him. I knew he was a tough customer and was in shape. But Vance would be out to help me soon. Maybe even Conti would help... no... Conti was in shock. He pissed his pants and was huddled in the corner like a scolded dog.

Gilheaney rolled me off with some jiu jitsu looking bullshit. He scored a blind punch that caught me on the chin. I fell back against the wheel. My bell was rung.

He wiped the goo out of his eyes and dove at me, bent over, driving three fast rabbit punches into my gut.

I dropped an elbow into his spine as hard as I could, but I must have missed. It just pissed him off. He raised up and head-butted me under the chin.

Where was Vance with the gun?

That's when I realized Nyx had completely blocked the hatch with his dead dumb ass. She was trapped below deck. Maybe I could buy some time for her to get out the ventilation hatch on the bow.

I doubled down on my effort in spite of feeling exhaustion coming on and being beat to hell by this asshole.

It was time to fight dirty. But I always fight dirty...full confession, I am getting my ass kicked and Gilheaney knows it.

I threw an anemic punch at his head. He slipped it and countered with a powerful knee strike to the nuts, which really pissed me off because I had recently been thinking of using them.

I slouched, weakened, and caught two stiff hooks to the side of the head.

Gilheaney saw I was beat and stepped away to pick up his gun.

He had me... then Vance appeared on the bow with the Benelli shotgun.

"Freeze asshole." She pointed the twelve-gauge at his head so he would know which asshole she was referring to.

He paused… smiled… and dropped the gun.

We were winning.

Then we weren't.

CHAPTER 11 - FIRST YOU SEE THEM, THEN YOU DON'T

I never heard the other boat, but it was on us quickly. I guess Vance didn't see it either before the floodlight blasted her in the face, temporarily blinding her.

"Nobody move." A voice I recognized shouted. I heard what sounded exactly like someone charging the chamber of an AR-15 rifle.

We were screwed. Even more than the last time I thought we were screwed. Fifteen miles out at sea in the dark. The weather taking a turn for the worse. I was beat to crap, Vance was blinded, and now we had two guns pointed at us.

I could barely breathe but I rasped out a greeting. "Hi Monica."

"Hi Becker. Are you ready to die?"

I gazed over at the beautiful red head... she was dressed in black capri pants and a black t-shirt. I noticed a red sash around her waist. She looked a little like a pirate. No, she looked a lot like a pirate with her hair blowing wildly in the breeze and her waving a dangerous weapon.

I knew we couldn't fight, so I tried talking. "You couldn't have picked a worse time, Monica... I have no interest in dying today."

She turned her attention to Joan. "Drop the shotgun, sugar, or I cut Becker in half.

Vance was cool. She dropped the M4 back down the hatch rather than tossing it over the side. Good job, Vance. You might still have a chance. I am pretty sure I am a dead man though.

Monica looked at Conti. "I need your account numbers and passwords. I assume they are on your phone, so open it up and give it to Gilheaney."

Conti, a shivering mess of fear, looked once at me desperately, then did as he was told.

Gilheaney took the phone and pushed some buttons. "We're good," he said with a grin. Apparently, they hit the motherlode.

I tried my last gambit. "You still don't have the storage locker full of cash."

I was talking to Monica, but Gilheaney butted in. "Yeah, and you don't either."

"In fact, I do... does the name Scarlett mean anything to you?"

"You know that name? How?"

"Remember the part about me being a detective?"

"Where is it, Becker."

"I'll tell you if you let us go... We won't talk."

Monica laughed out loud. "Really... you're going with that?"

I had to chuckle along with her. "Not a lot of cards left in the deck, baby."

She thought about it. She was still going to kill

us, but not right away. "Gilheaney raft me up with your boat." The money was too much for her to walk away from.

"What does that mean?" he asked.

"Tie the two boats together, side by side. Be ready to shoot though if they try something." She gave Vance and I a command. "Both of you get your hands high... don't try anything."

It was a reasonable order on her part, but trying something was the only shot we had for staying alive. So, at some point, we'd have to disobey that order. But not yet.

The inept sailor Gilheaney finally got the two boats tied off. We were now more like a barge than two sleek speedsters.

Monica came on board with the AR15 trained at my face. "Here's the deal, Becker. I might let your girlfriend Vance live if you give me the location now. But if you don't, I'll gut shoot her right off the deck."

I took a deep breath. "Mind if I have a smoke?"

It worked. I broke the momentum she was building up to kill us. She laughed.

"Sure, Becker. Have your last cigarette. I'm not cruel, just thorough."

I snugged a Lucky out of the pack and popped it in the corner of my mouth like I've done a thousand times. I slowly fished the SWAT zippo out of my pocket and lit it.

I offered her one.

"No thanks... I'm busy holding a gun."

I put the pack back in my pocket and took a long drag before I began.

"So, it was you all along..." I hoped she would start bragging. She didn't disappoint. Unlike Gilheaney, I think she felt like she needed to prove something. She wanted credit for her accomplishments. I sensed that deep down she was a neurotic psycho... she could have made a good HOA president had she not taken up a life of crime.

"Yeah, it was me. I killed Luca. I saw the value of the tech... I could have had that, control of the board, and all of the cash, but that asshole moved the money when he caught onto me. He accidentally died while I was trying to get him to tell me where it was."

"Then why kill Sonechka. She was your friend."

"Her? That piece of shit and her magic boyfriend? They were just cover. But she knew too much. Luca told her about his suspicions. He trusted her. He knew we were hanging out together and he tried to play detective. Things were getting out of control, so I hired Chen to clean up the mess. I guess you closed that loose end for me though, so thank you for that."

I took a long drag and blew a smoke ring to the Gods. "Yeah... you're welcome."

That got another snort out of her. I tried to keep it going. We needed a break, but I didn't see one for us in the immediate neighborhood yet.

The sea was getting a little rougher, not choppy yet, but something was coming. We might all die out here anyway if it gets ugly. The ocean is an unforgiving mistress and doesn't mind killing you at all. A light sprinkle started.

"Times up, Becker. What's the location?"

I noticed Gilheaney was quick glimpsing the sky. He was better on the water than Nyx was, but I think he was afraid of getting caught out here in a storm. His attention was divided, very slightly, but divided.

"Fine, I'll write it down. my logbook is write here. I'll tear a page out, write it down, then give it to Vance and she can leave with you. No sense in both of us dying."

"Sure, Becker. If that works for you."

She was lying. She was going to kill us both. What was stupid about it though, was that she *knew* that I knew.

I caught some movement out of the corner of my left eye. Conti... Good... it was time.

I looked around the helm for my logbook. "Where the hell?" I muttered. Then I shouted, "Vance, did you see my logbook down there on the chart table."

She picked up on my play, "Yeah."

The split second that Monica looked at her, I made my move. What they didn't realize that a cigarette break is my superpower. I felt pretty good after a quick rest. I wasn't just stalling, I was recharging my engine.

Poseidon was with us. The waves picked up and rocked the boat hard. More rain suddenly came down... this time it was serious. A crack of thunder drowned out all other sound and the wind whipped the rafted boats around like a carnival ride.

Sweeping with my right hand I pushed the barrel of the AR15 away from my kisser and did a Spartan kick, planted between Monica's boobs, sending her flying asshole over appetite back over the rail into her boat. Conti decided to be a man, which was a very positive development, and grabbed Gilheaney from behind in a bear hug, preventing him from plugging me. Vance dropped like a rock down the bow ventilation hatch. I throat punched Gilheaney with everything I had. His eyes crossed. I kicked him in the nuts hard. Real hard... then followed up with a punch in the snot locker that exploded his nose into a red grisly pulp of meat, snot, and blood.

As he collapsed on the deck, I stomped on his head.... ending his bullshit once and for all. It all happened in a split second, but that second was all Monica needed to return.

I looked up to see an AR15 pointed at me from the other boat. Monica's eyes were full of fire and rage... her hatred was palpable. She was going to kill me... she was going to kill us all. "Freeze

Becker. I don't need your.old fat ass... I'll find the money... I'm taking the casino myself. You're done, asshole."

Conti was freaking out. "Don't kill me, I'll help you. Please!"

I guess he relapsed into being a puss.

Monica stepped up on the gunwale and aimed the rifle at my face. "Goodbye, Becker."

There are times when you see your life flash before your eyes. Or at least I have been told that happens. All I saw before my eyes was the face of the devil, pure evil, a woman so ruthless she would murder anyone remotely in her way.

I raised a finger in the internationally recognized wait signal while I took a final drag off my smoke.

Her laughing eyes burned through me. Monica was laughing at my imminent death. She laughed at my hubris... then things changed.

Vance popped out of the hatch with my shotgun. "Hey, you red-headed bag of shit, stay the hell away from my man!"

Monica spun, but not fast enough.

The Benelli shotgun dumps a lot of lead downrange fast. I had it loaded with number four buckshot. That would do some damage at ten yards.

I watched Monica's face turn crimson and her head explode and spray across the deck of her boat as Vance pulled the trigger three times as fast as she could.

Vance was in warrior mode. She stomped across the decks and stood over Monica's body, unloading the rest of the shotgun into her twitching body. Then she pulled her AutoMag out of her belt and started to pump a round into the late Mister Gilheaney.

I stopped her. "He's dead and I don't need any holes in my boat, baby."

Our client started to stand up, not realizing Vance was still in warrior mode. His movement instinctively prompted her to point the big AutoMag at his kisser.

Conti screamed like a little girl... then composed himself... he looked at me, then Vance, and then sat down and said, "I think I shit my pants."

I expected Vance to still be in the kill zone, but she lowered her weapon, looked at him, and calmly said, "Don't worry about it. It's your first time at this. It gets easier."

She tossed the guns on the deck, grabbed me, and kissed me hard on the mouth. I let her.

A long minute later, she let me go. "Well, Becker, maybe you aren't too old for this kind of work after all."

I flopped back in the helm seat, exhausted. "Nah, I'm done. From now on, it's coffee on the deck in the morning, go to lunch, visit happy hour, then evening cocktails in the hot tub. I'm done."

She kissed me again. "Good call... Any final

orders, boss?"

"Yeah, see if we have a bottle of scotch and some clean glasses in the galley. I could use a drink."

"You got it."

Conti puked over the side... I think he'll be okay... some scotch will fix him right up.

Then the sky lit up...

A helicopter, two coast guard vessels, and a cigarette boat rolled up on us from out of nowhere, floodlights shining.

We were rescued.

Yay.

EPILOGUE

The final debriefing of me as the active leader of Becker Investigations was underway. After a quick check up by medics and a long investigation by the police, coast guard, and gambling commission, we were all finally back at the office together for the last time.

But I still had a few questions.

"So where did that cigarette boat come from?" I asked.

Worm explained, "When we saw things going south, Durd tried to buy a boat, any boat... but we weren't getting any response. Then he got a briefcase full of cash out of his van and waved it around. The guy with the cigarette boat bit. That cigarette boat crowd is kind of money driven anyway."

"What? Where did it come from?"

Durd answered, "It was some of Tiki's money."

"Tiki's money?"

Tiki gave me her pout face. She thinks it weakens me. It doesn't. Well, maybe a little.

Tiki answered. "I was going to tell you, Becker, I knew where the locker full of money was. I just forgot to mention it before. I only took two million."

Durd corrected her, "You took two hundred

thousand."

"Math not my thing."

I was confused. "When did you find the money?"

"Oh, I found it when you and I went to storage lockers. When I broke in office, I stole the disks with surveillance video on it. I see Luca moving big plastic tubs from his locker to the locker next to it. I went back and took some later."

"When?"

"Later."

"And you were going to tell me…"

"Later. You not my boss anymore, Becker. You can't do anything about it now. Tough shit, pal."

"Yeah, you got a point." I surrendered. There was no winning here.

Durd explained further. "I gave most of the recovered funds back to your friend Campbell to sort out. He's happy. He said this is all your fault but he's not arresting you this time…. or something like that."

"Good to know."

"Yeah, we kept the fee Monica agreed to before she turned evil and the cost of the cigarette boat."

"Seems fair. She probably won't complain."

Vance added, "Conti is happy. He paid us a two-hundred-and-fifty-thousand-dollar fee including bonus, for saving the casino and saving his life."

"Cool. So he's not suing us over the little misunderstanding at sea?"

"No, but he isn't going boating again anytime soon either."

There was a general chuckle around the room, then things got quiet. They knew why I called the meeting.

"So, this is it. We made a good score again. We're flush. All of you are officially on two weeks paid leave. Vance and I are..." I paused. I wasn't sure how to tell them. I didn't want to lose their respect by confessing I was engaging in a workplace romance with a younger woman. They might think less of me. I didn't want to disappoint them.

Durd made a weird face, "Becker, we were getting sick of her asking us if we thought you liked her. What kind of detective are you that you didn't pick up on it? Everyone else knew."

Tiki dove in, "I was going to be your girl if she didn't, Becker... Just out of pity. You are old and fat and just don't know. I don't know how any woman could like you. I show mercy... but not now... off the hook... that makes me happy."

"I'm what?"

She leaned in and gave me a kiss on the cheek then whispered in my ear, "I appreciate everything you've done for me, Becker. I am forever grateful."

What the hell? The diction of her whispered words was perfect, and she sounded like a midwestern English teacher. Dammit.. I knew she was faking that pigeon English accent...I needed a witness. "Did anyone else hear that?"

But no one else heard her. All I got was a wink from Tiki. I winked back. What else could I do. It was fun while it lasted.

Mister Worm stepped in to shake my hand, but he looked concerned. He asked, "Does this mean I need to find a new job?"

"No pal, it means you're working full time at the agency now. Welcome aboard." I shook his hand, then gave him a hug.

His grin almost split his face. "Thanks, boss."

All good guys have some 'criminal' in their blood, otherwise they wouldn't be able to do what it takes to be a good guy. But it is nice to see a bad guy turn it around. Worm was worth the investment. He's a good man.

I turned my attention to Nicolo, "Same for you, buddy. If you want a career change. We... uh, I mean, Vance could use you."

"I might do that, brother. I wouldn't mind being a part of this team. I don't know how to explain it, but without Sonechka, I'm not sure I want to go back and do the act alone...when they killed her, they killed the magic. So, I'll need some time before I decide to take you up on the offer. Maybe I'll take up fishing or something until I get my head straight." He closed his eyes a moment, gathered his thoughts, and then continued somberly. "Listen, I appreciate what you all did... each of you. Anything you ever need from me, just ask. I'll be there."

Then he hugged each of us... getting hugged by a traffic cop is unnerving... acting human had to be weird for him too.

I left...the room was silent. I breathed a deep sigh of relief as I walked out the door knowing I had a new stage of life to enter... and then I felt moisture on my cheek. Maybe it's sprinkling again.

FINALE

A week later, my boast was anchored just ten yards off the beach, bobbing in the gentle leeward waves. Just Joan and me, sipping our iced down beers and enjoying some sandwiches under the shade of a bright green canvas umbrella. A tiny uninhabited Caribbean island, a beautiful girl, and a cold beer.

As far as I'm concerned, Nicolo's greatest magic trick was dropping an ugly case into my lap that somehow turned into this moment of beauty.

Yeah, I'll take it.

No regrets.

THE END

ACKNOWLEDGEMENTS

Editorial support:
Randy Lewis
Magic inspiration
Carlo DeBlasio
Marketing and artistic support
Ryan Van Dyke
Paul Kennedy

Thank you all for your help. Any errors, typos, gun mistakes, magic errors, watch mistakes, boat mistakes, or weird stuff that doesn't make sense is on me, not the team.

ABOUT THE AUTHOR

Bronco Hammer

 Bronco Hammer is an author and artist who currently resides in Coronado, California. He is a retired Detective Lieutenant and a almost retired technology entrepreneur. His interests include boats, guns, cars, horses, and wristwatch collecting.

Stay in Touch
Bronco Hammer can be contacted to schedule interviews and book signings at www.broncohammer.com

BOOKS IN THIS SERIES

South Florida Mysteries
He's old, he's mean, and he carries a .45.
Private-eye Becker is a retired cop who lives in the little resort town of Lauderdale-by-the-Sea, Florida. As Becker tries to cope with the struggles of becoming a senior citizen, he still finds ways to apply his goon-squad style to solving cases.

A Walk Down Bullet Alley

Becker, an aging ex-cop turned private investigator has a dead former client, a mysterious note, and rumors of a missing forty million dollars. Now a bunch of unwelcome Californians are on the scene, screwing up Becker's Florida.

Dead As Hell In Fort Lauderdale

Wealthy retired cop Becker lives an idyllic life in his waterfront Lauderdale-by-the-Sea Florida home... until a random acquaintance from his past is murdered by radiation poisoning. Spies, cartel kingpins, and corrupt government agents muddy the waters as Becker tries to find the killer. Yeah, it's just another day in Florida.

The Magic Killers

When magician Nicolo DeCarlo's assistant goes missing, he calls his old friend Becker, a Fort Lauderdale private investigator. But finding the missing woman is one thing, having random hoods, thugs, and criminals trying to kill you is something else. Especially if you don't know why.

CHARACTERS WHO APPEARED IN OTHER BOOKS

Becker previously appeared in:
- A Walk Down Bullet Alley
- Dead as Hell in Fort Lauderdale

Joan Vance previously appeared in:
- Dead Guy in the Alley; A Love Story
- Murder Every Maggot
- A Walk Down Bullet Alley
- Dead as Hell in Fort Lauderdale

Worm previously appeared in:
- A Walk Down Bullet Alley
- Dead as Hell in Fort Lauderdale

Tommy from Lauderdale previously appeared in:
- A Walk Down Bullet Alley
- Dead as Hell in Fort Lauderdale

Mr. Stump (referenced in The Magic Killers)
- Dead Guy in the Alley; a Love Story
- I Stomp on your Throat
- Murder Every Maggot
- A Walk Down Bullet Alley

June Glume
  • June Gloom

BOOKS BY BRONCO HAMMER

SoCal Noir Detective Stories
Hollywood Scum Must Pay Spank Me
JCPI
Pimps Must Die
Die You Commie Bastards
Generation Two - SoCal Noir Detective Stories
I Stomp on your Throat
Dead Guy in the Alley, A Love Story
Murder Every Maggot
Random Violence
See You in Hell
Die You Filthy Animal
Man of Violence
June Gloom
Narc in the Dark
South Florida Mysteries
A Walk Down Bullet Alley
Dead as Hell in Fort Lauderdale
The Magic Killers
Friendship Foundation Books
Die You Slimy Maggot
Deep State Deadly
Science Fiction
Assholes from Space